THE GREEN FELLA

Sgt. Collins R.I.C.

By

David McCann

Peach Orchard Publishing
ISBN-13: 978-1-5272-8108-0

CONTENTS

PROLOGUE

Frankie McPhilips, a large, heavy farmer, wasn't built for running but this morning he had had a reason to run, he was being followed by men in dark trench coats. He couldn't see their faces from this distance, but he had already been close enough to them to know that they were up to no good on this dark Ulster night. He stumbled and fell face down in the cold brown mud, then he struggled to his feet, his heart bursting with fear, and ran, his run across the icy Tyrone countryside had left him both exhausted and terrified. *Somebody is after me and following me,* he thought. At 43 years old he was in no fit state to walk across the fields never mind having to run for his life. His decision to venture out to check on his cattle had put him in possible danger. Peering into the darkness of the still November night he could see nothing, but he knew that his pursuers were not far away.

Dirty wet clinging mud hung from his coat and trousers, it stuck to every part of him, weighing him down in the very moment of his escape. Voices echoed from a nearby forest, his hunters were searching for him. Frankie crouched frozen in fear, listening to the sounds of danger. *I must get out of here*, he thought.

With all the strength he had left in his fatigued body he stood up and tried to run some more, but each step he took was painful and he stumbled and fell again and again. He lost a boot in the escape from the chase and his right foot was bare cold and bleeding. Lying down on the wet grass Frankie felt like a fox being hunted by the hounds and the hounds will soon catch up with him. He needed to rest his exhausted body but he didn't have the time to do it. Rising from his hiding place Frankie crouched down slightly so his pursuers couldn't see much of his silhouette against the night sky. He could hear his heart pounding in his chest, it was so loud he thought that it might be heard by the men hunting him and give him away.

Taking a big deep breath to push himself some more he ran across the top of the field as quick as possible, he then battled on again across streams, ditches, through hedges, and along frost-crusted lanes until he reached the cottage and home.

"Thanks be to Jesus, I made it," he said as he collapsed through the front door. Tired and still frightened but at least he was safe behind the strong stone wall. Once inside Frankie bandaged up his bleeding foot and crawled under the warm blankets on his heavy iron bed, he wrapped himself around the sheet tightly in the foetal position and squeezed the grey wool blanket over his head and chest. His fear fought to keep him awake but the tiredness fought back and battled with his alert mind to make him sleep. In the end, the tired part won and took over and he just drifted off into a deep, comfortable sleep in relative peace, but, as it turns out, he was far from being safe.

CHAPTER ONE

SIXMILECROSS, IRELAND

21ST NOVEMBER 1920, 3.30 A.M.

Thud, bang, knock. "Police on duty! Open the door or we will break it down!"

The heavy wooden door vibrated with fury and the early morning silence was broken by the loud knocking sounds of the dreaded Irish knock on the door, it drifted and echoed across the countryside. Elderly Mrs McPhilips is also disturbed by the heavy sounds at her bedroom window, startled she peers out of her curtains in absolute terror. "Who is there at this time of night?" she asks softly in a frightened voice.

"Police on duty," came the loud reply, men in dark coats carrying rifles and wearing Police caps stood staring back at the terrified old woman. "Is your son Frankie home?" they asked with menace.

"Yes, he is," she said.

"Tell him to get dressed and come out now or we'll break your cottage door down."

Frankie limped out of bed, his foot was still sore from the earlier barefoot escape, it's not the same men who chased after him earlier he thought, it's the Police. He opened the door knowing he was safe and he was ready to tell them of the earlier chase.

"Mother stay in the house, I will be back shortly," he reassured her, he hugged and then kissed her on the forehead. "Stay here, I will be fine. I will be back soon." His mother stood and said nothing, she was in a state of shock, he stepped outside and his fear returned when a pistol was pushed under his chin and the men threw a some punches at him, a lamp light was shone in his face.

"Are you Frankie McPhilips?" he was asked.

"I am," he said.

"What age are you?"

"43," he replied. They kicked him a few times on his shins and thighs.

"What were you doing talking to the Priest from the village today?"

"I have never spoke to anybody all evening."

"That's not what we have been told. Are you a Papist?" one man growled.

"Yes," replied Frankie.

"Well, that's all we need to know, you are coming with us!" Frankie was handcuffed and marched by the men down the path to a waiting motor car. You can see the look of terror in his eyes as he meekly clambers into the back of the car and is driven away. His mother stands at the front door of the cottage and watches as the car speeds down the lane and vanishes into the darkness.

SIXMILECROSS, IRELAND

21ST OF NOVEMBER 1920, 7.00 A.M.

Sergeant Patrick Joseph Collins of the Royal Irish Constabulary, born in Dunmanway, County Cork, 17th of August 1872. Sgt. 60722 aged 48 in 1920

Sgt. Collins stood staring at the gun rack. Eight brown Lee Enfield rifles stood upright, polished, clean, and ready for use. From the holster on his Police issue belt he produced a Webley revolver and counted out rounds of ammunition, he placed his firearm back in the holster when he was satisfied the pistol was clean, in working order, and ready for use. A familiar sound made him peer out the top floor window of the police barracks, a Crossley tender car turned into the main street of the village, white clouds of fumes spluttered from the Crossley's rear exhaust as it made its way with purpose towards the grey commanding building of the barracks. The barracks was a large impressive two-storey grey stone building with an attic and a slate roof standing out at right angles to the main street, its steep steps rose up sharply to meet the big heavy wooden door. Sgt. Collins looked at his watch, 7 a.m., the Crossley is on time, he thought. He watched as three green clad Policemen clambered from the motor vehicle and walked towards the main door of Sixmilecross Barracks, another Constable remained behind in the car, ever alert to danger he sat in the front passenger seat, his Lewis machine gun rested on the main dashboard, always at the ready for the slightest hint of trouble. He went downstairs to meet Inspector O'Callahan.

"Welcome to the barracks, Inspector, make yourself at home. My men are ready for inspection, but first I have to make an unexpected call to the McPhilips home just outside the village, her son was taken away in the middle of the night by armed men and has not been seen since." He showed the Inspector and Constables into the small cramped Sergeants' Office which was tidy but piled high with paperwork. The sign on the door said SGT. P.J.C. so the Inspector knew just who it belonged to. "Sorry about the condition of my office, you know that the Head Constable in charge of the barracks is still in Hospital?"

"Yes I know, we will try and get a replacement as soon as possible." Sgt. Collins didn't respond to Inspector O'Callahan's remark.

"Sir I have got to go out to the McPhilips home and find out what has happened."

He turned to the two Constables at the front desk. "Constable Foley and Constable Cullinan, could one of you go and tell the new fellow Constable Whelan to get our bicycles and meet me at the front door?"

"Yes sir," said Foley. He spun around quickly and walked out to the small walled parade ground at the back of the barracks where the rest of the police officers stood at ease waiting for Inspection. "Constable Whelan can you collect two bicycles and meet Sgt. Collins at the front door?" said Foley. Whelan didn't speak, he just stepped out of the thin green parade line and, with his boots crunching the gravel ground, he set off for the bicycles and brought them to the main door. Sgt. Collins stepped outside.

"Constable Whelan we are going out to the McPhilips cottage to investigate the disappearance of a male member from the homestead, we won't need the car and we won't need our rifles until later so we will just bring our revolvers."

Constable Whelan looked concerned at this order. "Yes Sergeant," he said reluctantly.

"We will be fine," said Sgt. Collins. "I have no intelligence to indicate that the Volunteers are operating this morning in this part of Tyrone."

"If that was who took Frankie McPhilips last night

they will be long gone."

"I hope," said Sgt. Collins with a brave smile, he wasn't worried about what danger could be waiting but Constable Whelan was, as he nervously smiled back he wasn't quite as sure as his Sgt. was. Collins barked an order through the open door to Constable Cullinan at the front desk. "Cullinan bring the men in from the Parade ground and make them wait inside, its cold outside and myself and Whelan could be gone a long time at this call." Cullinan jumped up and ran out to the Parade ground, both men mounted their bicycles and rode up the muddy main road of the Village on the Tiroony Road past the red-bricked railway station. Collins spoke to Whelan as they both cycled. "You have been only here a week or so, Constable Whelan, how are you finding things?"

"It's grand, everything is fine," he answered. Sgt. Collins eyes scanned the road ahead; he wasn't nervous but it was right to check who was in front of them as "You can never be too careful in these times" he said. Maybe leaving the rifles behind wasn't such a good idea after all, he thought, but he tried to reassure the Constable in his company.

"So you're from Dublin, what part are you from, Constable Whelan?"

"Druncondra," came the sudden reply. "You also have a Dublin accent, Sgt. Collins, but I thought you were from Cork?"

"Yes I was born in Dunmanway County Cork on the 17th of August 1872," said Sgt. Collins in great detail, Whelan listened and also watched the road ahead, it was a lot of information but that was Sgt. Collins. He continued with his story; "My family moved to Dublin when I was two years old. My Father got work in a big brewery and left the farm to my older brother to work, that is why I have a Dublin accent but I am actually from Cork. I'm also a widower, my wife died in 1910, God rest her, and my seven children are all grown up now so I don't see them much."

"Well, sure they've their own lives to live."

"Five of them live in Cork, that's another reason to get back home. My long-term plan is to transfer back to an RIC Barracks anywhere in Cork as soon as a transfer becomes available, but I suppose it could be next week or next year, then I will finish my Police work in Tyrone. My hope is to get stationed in Dunmanway Barracks in Cork but Macroom, Bandon, Clonakility, or Roscarberry Barracks would all be fine for me. I would also hope to be promoted to Head Constable, but if I got a move staying at my present rank of Sergeant, then I would accept that too, as long as I get back to my home county. I've worked all over Ireland in my career," said Collins. "I joined the RIC in 1892 when I was 20 years old, I have worked in Dundalk, Co Louth, Salthill in Galway, Bundoran in Donegal, and Ballyvaughan in County Clare before coming up on the train to Enniskillen, where I worked in Enniskillen Barracks in Belmore Street for a year, then I came here to Sixmilecross in 1918 which will, I hope, be my second last job before getting back to Cork.

"I will also be able to help my brother on the farm in Dunmanway and I have already sent my transfer papers to RIC Headquarters in Phoenix Park, Dublin, and have been accepted for the move, but my job is here in Tyrone until then." Collins paused briefly before looking at Whelan. "Is this your first time out of Dublin?"

"Yes I was working in Limerick Barracks but was sent here, I have never been to Ulster before."

"Well, you'll find Ulster no different to the rest of Ireland, Whelan, it's the same job as everywhere else. I have had three postings in Ulster myself – Bundoran, Enniskillen, and now here in Sixmilecross." They cycled a little faster to warm their bodies on this cold morning but at least it was dry and the rain stayed away. The two officers reached the crime scene to find Mrs McPhilips standing on the well-scrubbed door step waiting for them; a cold breeze blew through her black woollen shawl, the air was chilled on this cold November morning. Sgt. Collins shook the old lady's hand.

"We have come about the disappearance of your son. I need to ask you some questions, can we go inside out of the cold?" Mrs McPhilips blows her already reddish nose on her clothing, she had been crying recently and her eyes were also red. They go inside the cottage; it was slightly cold as no fire had been lit yet. Mrs McPhilips had more to worry about than a fire this morning. She sat down on the hard, wooden chair next to the unlit grate. Collins and Whelan stood directly in front of her; both men, at six-foot tall, towered over the seated woman like giants and had their notebooks open, pencils in hand, ready to write. "Can you tell me what happened to your son early this morning, Mrs McPhilips?" She stared into space for a moment, trying to remember the events of the night before which had brought two Policemen to her door this grey cold morning.

"I heard loud knocking at the front door around three or four o'clock this morning, I can't really remember the time but it was somewhere in between those times." The two officers were writing down what she was saying. "I was very frightened but they said they were Police on duty. Frankie, my son, got dressed and opened the door, they hit him in the face and grabbed him by the shirt collar and took him outside to a car and that was it, he was gone, it was all over so quickly." Collins studied his notebook.

"How many men were there and what were they

wearing?" he asked.

"It was so dark; I think there was four or six men in black coats and caps, but it was oh so dark and I was too scared to look much at them."

Whelan spoke, "Did your son have any enemies or somebody he might have had an argument with?" He peered down at her intently.

"Not that I know of," she replied. "He didn't have an enemy in the world, he just worked on the farm and that was it. Frankie never went out to the pub to drink, he just worked and slept. The men also asked him was he a Catholic and what was he doing with the village Priest." Collins stood and stared intently, that sounds very strange, he thought.

"Mrs McPhilips," he said, "the Police will set up an investigation to find your son. I will call out to the cottage later on today myself to gather some more information, so if you can think of anything more about last night at all it really would be helpful. I will give you a few hours to try and remember, we will be back later on today." She nodded her head in silence, got up, and walked to the door.

"Thank you both," she said. Collins and Whelan left the house and walked towards their bicycles ready for the return cycle ride back to the barracks. As they rode away both men discussed the situation.

"What do you think happened, sir?" said Whelan.

"It doesn't look good, Whelan, this is happening all over Ireland, we are living in bad times, bad times, hopefully we can find him."

"God will help," said Whelan, Collins laughed.

"I go to mass every Sunday and I'm a Catholic but sometimes I wonder if we just die and that's it, we are born on a certain date and we die on a certain date and between those dates is all we get, maybe we don't have a soul at all, we could just be only shadows passing time. One day, all we will be is faded old photos on our great-, great-grandchildren's parlour room wall, we will be dead, gone, and forgotten." As Whelan listened Collins spoke grimly, "Life's not fair and that's it."

CHAPTER TWO

The green Police line stood waiting in the walled parade ground at the back of the barracks for Sgt. Collins and County Inspector O'Callahan; Collins and Whelan arrived back from their investigation.

"Constable Whelan take the two bicycles and put them away in the shed, and then join the rest of the men in line for the inspection," he said.

"Yes Sir," said Whelan, he put the bicycles away and then he marched into line. Collins walked along the line of his men.

"Right!" he barked, "go inside and get your rifles before the main inspection starts and come straight back out here." The men trooped off to the gun rack and collected the firearms, then made it back to their positions as before. Collins went inside to show O'Callahan around the inside of the building. There was a monthly inspection by the District Inspector but today was the quarterly inspection by the County

Inspector. The men stood and watched as the two officers went from room to room in the barracks. Every room they entered was clean and in order, especially the sleeping quarters, the bedding was clean and neatly folded on the bedsteads in military fashion. The bedding was made up of a straw mattress and a bolster with a good supply of blankets and a top covering, feather pillows were not permitted. The constables' kit were examined, this kit consisted of a suit of plain clothes, a pair of shoes, shirt, socks, towel, shaving equipment, and a square bar of soap as well as a knife, fork, and spoon.

"Excellent," said O'Callahan, "everything upstairs in the sleeping quarters is fine, we will go downstairs to check the records books." Collins said nothing, he was satisfied with the work he and the men had done. The records book sat on the front desk waiting to be inspected. O'Callahan picked up each one in turn – the station notebook, the patrol book, the order book and then he looked at the postage book, warrant book, and lost property book, all of which were in order. O'Callahan was pleased with what he saw.

"Great job, Collins, we shall go outside now and inspect the men." The six constables stood in line as Collins spoke to them.

"Stand to attention, no talking in the ranks; I will introduce County Inspector O'Callahan to who you all are. This is Constable Ignatius Foley from Co Kerry,

Constable Matthew Jennings from Co Tipperary, next to him is Constable Jonathan Fennell from Co Waterford and Constable Liam Whelan from Dublin, Constable Tobias Cullinan from Co Wexford and Constable Michael Flaherty from Co Westmeath." O'Callahan nodded and said nothing, he walked up and down the parade line and minutely scrutinized everyone, they were all clean shaven with their hair cut short, uniform, arms, and appointments were all clean and well fitting. The leather parts were all polished to shine with the steel parts glittering and free from any rust.

"Well done men, you all look splendid, you are a credit to the force, this part of the duty is over, thank you." He then went back inside, leaving Collins standing proudly with his men.

"Well done men, you have made me very pleased this morning but it's not over yet, the inspector coming from Omagh today was only part of the job." The men looked at each other. "Constable Foley I want you to go on to the front desk now, you will stay in the barracks, the rest of you I want you outside in the Crossley Tender." They all left the parade ground and took their positions as Collins ordered.

CHAPTER THREE

Three Crossley Tenders drove up the steep mountain road near the beautiful hillside area of Gortin Glen Forest which is situated at the foot of the Sperrin Mountains in County Tyrone, six policemen sat in each car, tightly holding their rifles with both hands, the butt of their weapons were pressed against the floor of the truck, the gun barrel pointing skywards. Bandoliers were slung across their heavy-issue great coats. Collins and his men were in the second car, they had stopped at Beragh and Omagh RIC Barracks to meet the other two cars and the rest of the constables, then they were travelling on to Gortin Barracks to meet the last of the policemen of the raiding party. Nobody knew what was planned for this morning, Collins didn't know either.

"We will be told when we get there," he hissed to one of his officers who had the audacity to ask the question. The convoy made its way towards Gortin Barracks along the winding country roads, as they travelled the men pulled up the collars of their great coats to keep out the cold wind in the open-topped motor car.

"Sgt. we need a charrabang for this job today," said Whelan, "at least they are covered and not exposed to the elements."

Collins stared at him, "I agree," he said, "but I can't see HQ in Dublin doing anything to help, we have to make do with what we have here at our disposal and that's that, now no more talking in the ranks until we get to our last stop." The convoy arrived at Gortin Barracks, the cars growling as they made their way into the village. A fourth crossley was parked outside waiting for them. "Alright men get out of the car," Collins shouted. "We will do another quick inspection before we find out what the job is." Eighteen police constables stood to attention on Gortin's main street outside the barracks. They were ready for whatever their orders were for today; this was serious, thought Collins, for now the District Inspector was also present along with three more sergeants and County Inspector O'Callahan. The sergeant walked down the line of men.

"Right boys check you have everything with you that you will need: your rifle, pistol, ammunition, truncheon, handcuffs, and whistle." Everything was in order so the District Inspector then briefed his men on what the job was for this morning.

"Under the illicit distillation act of 1831 subsection 4 it is illegal to have on the said person or persons equipment that can be used to produce any spirits and under section 25 which relates to the movement of stills or spirits of the 1831 act."

Collins then spoke up; "In other words, we have received information that somebody is making poteen in the Gortin Glen area, and it is up to us to find them. Now it's a big area but we have a fairly good idea where we should look. What we need to look out for is a still pot, still head, copper worm, and arm, the brew is made with barley, sugar, water, and yeast. You are going to be equipped with long, pointed steel rods, and will be using them for probing haystacks and corn stacks, that is where the illicit poteen stills will be hiding." Collins stubbed his boots into the hard ground, he looked down at his action then looked up again at the men. "80 years ago a company of red coated Yeomanry called the Gortin Imperial Yeomanry patrolled this area and their principal duty was to search for illicit spirits and poteen stills, today it is the men of the Royal Irish Constabulary doing the searching, good luck and by gods help we will all be safe. Now lads the history lesson is over, get back on board the Crossleys now."

The men all got back into the motor cars ready for the journey to the forest.

CHAPTER FOUR

SIXMILECROSS, IRELAND

21ST NOVEMBER 1920

Sgt. Collins and his men made their way across the heavily wooded hillside of Gortin Glen, also present was County Inspector O'Callahan, he was never bothered about mucking in and getting his hands or feet dirty, but the rest of the officers decided to stay by the warm turf fire of Gortin Barracks. "Right men, we have come through the trees without finding anything, we are going to sweep the hillside and check those haystacks and anything that looks out of the ordinary." Their rifles were slung over their backs in a casual manner as they made their way down the large sloping meadow. "Spread out in a long line and use your metal rods to check for stills."

"Ah fer fuck sake," said Whelan, "the field is full of cow shite." Constable Flaherty laughed.

"Ya big Dublin gobshite you have never been out of the city in yer life, it's a field, of course it's going to be full of cow shite," he said.

"Be very careful where you put your feet as I don't want the smell of shite in the car all the way home," said Whelan as he surveyed his next step. All the men laughed as they carefully trudged around the sometimes brown circular cow pats, it was a cold winter's day so nobody knew if the ground was solid to walk on or if they might end up ankle deep in the dung if it was too fresh. Every haystack that stood in the pasture was prodded for the hidden stills that the Constables had come to find, but so far nothing remotely to do with Poteen could be found. Having crossed the field, they came to a stop at the edge of a hedgerow. "Check in here, men," instructed Collins, they reached in with their metal prods and poked the bushes from top to bottom.

It was easy to see into the winter undergrowth and again nothing was found. Collins wasn't perturbed. "We will look somewhere else, get back in the cars and we'll drive to another location." The Crossleys rumbled down the road that was in the middle of the forest, the tall trees were on each side of the motor car. Collins looked from side to side and turned to and spoke to O'Callahan. "It's a great place for an ambush, Inspector," he said. O'Callahan bit his lip and looked slightly worried.

"Yes, it certainly is," he said nervously. As the car reached halfway down the forest road Collins reached over to the driver and squeezed his shoulder lightly.

"Stop the car I need to get out and take a piss," he said. The car stopped and Collins went up by the nearest grass bank towards the privacy of the trees. As he peered down the bank, he could see white wisps of smoke rising from the forest floor. We have found what we come for, he thought. He took out his police whistle from his top pocket, turned towards his men, and blew into the mouthpiece. Its sharp shrill noise made the men jump up in their seats, they all got out of the car and ran towards him. "Form a column and follow me, men," ordered Collins. The green line made its way towards the forest trail. When the men reached the origin of the smoke it was obvious that they had indeed found what they were looking for, a big forty gallon copper pot stood in the clearing, whoever had been using it was gone, but the wet turf that was being used to heat the liquid had gave away the stills position. The copper pot had a wooden cap which had a copper arm; it was inserted between the cap and the copper worm. This was a coil of copper tubing that was placed in a wooden vat and sealed around the edges with porridge.

Collins smiled, "Oh since its perfection, no doctor's direction, can cleanse the complexion like poteen my boys." His face lit up with satisfaction. "Right men spread out and see if anybody is hiding nearby, they couldn't have gone too far."

A few minutes later Constable Flaherty arrived back to the still with two men he had found hiding behind a tree, he walked them towards the Inspector. Foley had his pistol out, pointing at their backs. They walked with their hands up and didn't speak.

"Does any of the Gortin Constables know these men?" said Collins.

"Yes," said a constable. "That's the Mc Loughlin brothers from the village, they are known to us for making poteen."

"What are you two men doing up here?" said O'Callahan.

"Ah sir we just came for the fresh air sure there's no harm in that," said one of them smugly.

"Handcuff them and take them back to the barracks and seize everything that's here," said O'Callahan. Both men were marched to the car and another Crossley had to traverse the hillside to reach the place where the still was sitting, with great difficulty it was then placed into the back of the car and the convoy set off for Gortin Barracks; this is where the two Mc Loughlin brothers would be locked away in their cells. The poteen still and all its working parts were also locked away as evidence. "We will have both of them up in front of the R.M. in Omagh petty sessions court first thing on Monday morning, but proving that they were making poteen will be another matter," said Inspector O'Callahan. "However, we confiscated somebody's equipment and disrupted their supply so it's a job well done."

The policemen sat smoking and drinking tea at the blazing fire, pleased with the job they had done and even more pleased to be back in the warmth of the building again.

CHAPTER FIVE

SIXMILECROSS, IRELAND

21ST NOVEMBER 1920

At 2 p.m. Sgt. Collins and his six constables arrived back in their own village as they all walk through the front door of the barracks. Constable Foley is stood behind the front desk; his face ashen and grim. "What is wrong?" asked Collins.

"I have three things to report, Sgt., you must deal with this one first: Lord Basil Copeland telephoned and said that he wants to speak to you personally about the matter, the poachers were back last night and he has had pheasants taken and salmon have been netted from the stream that runs through his land. He wants to know what the police are doing about it." Collins listened. "The second incident; somebody stopped the train before it reached the station and ransacked the mailbags from it, the train is now with the stationmaster, and he is waiting for us to go down and investigate what happened, and third, well, there have been multiple shootings all over Dublin this morning. We think about ten intelligence

G men have been shot dead in their beds."

"Headquarters plan to send a party of police, Auxiliaries, and Black and Tans to a football match taking place this afternoon at Croke Park to arrest any gunmen attending the game."

Collins and his men looked shocked at what was going on in Dublin but there was nothing they could do about it. "Leave your rifles back in the gun rack, our pistols will be enough. Constable Whelan and Jennings when you do that, walk down to the railway station and find out what is going on. I'm going out to Lord Copeland's estate to find out about the poaching, Constable Cullinan will join me and we will take our bicycles." All four hurried off to investigate their selected incidents. The last two constables were sent on a foot patrol around the village. "We need to be patrolling and seen in the village patrolling," he said.

Lord Basil Copeland stood waiting at the large front door of his Country estate home, it was built by his great-grandfather in 1820 on the ruins of the family's Plantation Castle which stood on the same site since 1615. He stood smoking a cigarette and wearing his red scarlet fox hunters jacket, black boots, and white britches; in his other hand he held a riding crop and foxhunter's horn. Waiting for Sgt. Collins to arrive he surveyed his empire within an empire, and it was impressive, the house stood in two thousand acres of rolling parkland, a neo-Tudor mansion with turrets and crenelated towers reaching onto the sky. As Collins approached, he could see Lord Copeland's thin wiry frame and his small weasel-like face standing staring back at him.

"Good afternoon Sergeant," he said formally in his clipped Anglicized accent. Collins got off his bicycle.

"Afternoon sir, this is Constable Cullinan." All three men shook hands. "You telephoned earlier that the poachers have come back."

"Indeed, I did, Sgt.," he said. Lord Copeland stood on the Portland stone steps looking down at the two policemen. "I honestly don't think there is a lot you can do about the situation as your men are stretched to the limit with everything that is going on in Ireland at the moment." Collins looked confused.

"Why did you ask us to come out here then if you thought we couldn't do anything about it?"

Lord Copeland drew on his cigarette and paused slightly, once again he surveyed his estate and what he had achieved. "I can't sit doing nothing anymore so I have decided to help you out."

"How do you mean?" said Collins.

"I had a group of law-abiding men working for me called Tyrone Vigilance, now they have been sworn in as constables in a new force called the Ulster Special Constabulary, they will be here to help you. The

Reverend Samuel Smythe is taking tea in my drawing room now, he has sworn them in this morning on the good book." He took the foxhunting horn he was holding and blew into it.

As the loud noise from the horn bellowed a Crossley motor car drove into view up the gravel road towards the men and stopped next to them, a small union jack flag flew on the front of the car and a large red hand of Ulster crest was painted on the bonnet and written above the sign was 'Roaring Meg'. Lord Copeland's family crest was displayed on both car doors.

"Sgt. Collins and Constable Cullinan I want you to meet Roaring Meg and my men, all from Ulster and all from Tyrone. This is Special Constable William Laird from Fintona, Special Constable Cecil Morton from Omagh, Special Constable Charles Wilson from Dromore, Special Constable Fredrick Lewis from Trillick, Special Constable George Mills from Beragh, Special Constable James Coulter from Sixmilecross and their Sergeant Robert Hall from Fivemiletown."

Collins and Cullinan reached over to shake the newly sworn in Special Constables hands, but they declined the offer, this created a slightly frosty atmosphere between both parties. Lord Copeland smirked a little. "Now, now, men," he said, "after all, we are all wearing the king's uniform." Reluctantly the Specials extended their arms and everyone eventually shook hands. Collins stared intently at the new uniforms they wore, every single piece of equipment which the RIC had they had too; a Crossley tender car, Lewis gun rifles and pistols, all to match, and a strange black uniform.

"Where did you get the uniforms and equipment from, Lord Copeland?"

He smiled, "Oh just a quick telephone call to my old regiment and they supplied all, the uniforms are just Army khaki battledress dyed black, the cap badge is the same as yours – a harp and crown insignia." Collins looked a little shocked.

"Lord Copeland did you not receive the letter when you asked about creating a constabulary from Dublin Castle refusing that request and they suggested instead supplying your men with whistles and caps for summoning the RIC?" Lord Copeland rocked his head back and he and his men roared and shook with laughter.

"Yes we did receive that letter and our response to it was Dublin Castle can go to hell from now on as we will look after ourselves." Collins and Cullinan both frowned.

"I'm sorry Lord Copeland but we must get back to the village, we have another job to take care of."

Lord Copeland agreed, "Yes I know all about the train and I think today was a good day to create a new

Constabulary. I've heard that more than ten British officers have been murdered in their beds in Dublin this morning."

Collins looked bemused, "How did you find about this, sir?" he asked. Lord Copeland looked amused.

"My dear Sergeant, you don't honestly think that we set up a Constabulary without an intelligence gathering operation, do you? We will operate independently from the RIC but we will be here to help, my men are billeted in the summer house on my estate so I won't need to bother you about poachers again."

"Alright then," said Collins. "We shall leave now, we need to get to the railway station right away."

"Thank you for coming, Sgt. I won't keep you any longer. Now, if you will excuse me, I'm going fox hunting shortly." Lord Copeland always had to get the last word in, his point was proved. The two men got back on their bicycles and went back out the gates towards the village.

CHAPTER SIX

SIXMILECROSS, IRELAND

21ST NOVEMBER 1920

Lord Basil Copeland stood with his men and watched the two policemen cycle down the gravel road towards the main gate of his estate. The Reverend Samuel Smythe emerged from the house just in time to see them disappear around the trees, he slinked towards the party of men. The Reverend was a large framed man with greying hair and a sharp face. He spoke with a strong, harsh voice;

"I'm just in time to see them leave with their tails between their legs," he chortled.

"How do you know they have tails, Reverend?" asked Special Constable Coulter.

"Well for a start all Papists have tails," he bellowed, "and horns too, being that they are the devils spawn." Everyone roared with laughter. "It might be funny to all of you, but I don't care if he is wearing the king's uniform, he is still a pope-head and I don't trust him or his constables."

"Where is he from, Basil?"

"He is from Cork but he speaks with a Dublin accent," said Lord Copeland.

"So he is from Cork and his name is Collins, well he must be related to that rebel gunman and murderer Michael Collins," said the Reverend. Lord Copeland agreed.

"I'm going to give him a nickname," he said, "we will call him the Green Fella as the Royal Irish Constabulary are known as the Green Fellows and gunman Michael Collins is called the big fella."

"A rather fitting name indeed, now shall we have some tea before you go hunting?" said the Reverend.

"What a good idea," replied Lord Copeland. "Alright men I want you to do a patrol of the estate and if you see any poachers shoot them and we'll just say we thought they were rebels, and don't worry about the Green Fella and his friends in Dublin Castle, we will do our own thing from now on."

*

Collins and Cullinan cycled towards the village, they were going quite fast as they were trying to reach the railway station to find out who had stopped the train and removed the mailbags.

"What was that all about at the Lord's house, sir?" asked Cullinan.

"They were trying to humiliate us and the RIC," he said. "Lord Basil Copeland is a member of the Anglo-Irish aristocracy and the Protestant ascendancy, he served in the British Army with the 15 hussars as a second lieutenant during the great war of 1914–1918 and won the military cross at the battle of loos and the French awarded him the Croix de Guerre. He retired in 1919 as rank of Captain and came home to farm his estate. He is anti-Catholic and he is good friends with the Reverend Samuel Smythe, who we didn't meet but they both have a big say in this part of the country. Both men have friends in high places in unionist circles. In fact, when Edward Carson visits Tyrone he stays with Lord Copeland at the estate."

"So who is this new Constabulary, Sgt. Collins?" said Cullinan.

"They started out maybe 10 years ago as the Ulster Volunteers then they became the Ulster Volunteer force to oppose home rule, then the great war started in 1914 and they became the Ulster Division. They went back to being the UVF in 1918 after the war was over, and now in 1920 they have become the Ulster Special Constabulary. My point is they are the same men with the same agenda only they use different names. I think the whole situation is getting out of control, we now have five police forces operating in Ireland; there is us, The Royal Irish Constabulary, the Auxiliary Division of the RIC, another force is called the Black and Tans by the rebels, and the Irish Republican police, which is operating in twenty two of Ireland's thirty two counties and now the Ulster Special Constabulary.

"We are reaching a very dangerous situation," said Collins.

"It's a worrying time indeed, Sgt.," said Constable Cullinan. "Why is the Crossley called Roaring Meg?"

Collins looked at him. "It is named after one of the canons which stood guard on the walls of Derry during the siege of 1688. King William of Orange came and saved the Protestants who were under siege by King James' Catholic army. That canon, Roaring Meg, defended the Protestants who protected the city."

"Yes I understand now, sir, that car will do the same job as the canon if the rebels attack." Collins nodded but didn't speak as both men knew what this would mean in the months to come. They soon arrived at the railway station to find out what was happening from the constables who had reached the scene earlier.

CHAPTER SEVEN

SIXMILECROSS, IRELAND

SATURDAY 11TH SEPTEMBER 1920

Standing at the window of the barracks on a cold November day, Sgt. Collins looked down at the newly erected barbed wire entanglements around the front door; also, the looped holed steel plates and the sandbags that protected the windows. "This is not a police building anymore, it's an army barracks in the frontline of a war," he said. As he stood and stared at the barricades, his mind took him back to a day only a few months ago when possibly, for the last time, he could claim to be a policeman. Yes, a policeman that you would find in the Scottish Highlands or a Bobby on the beat in London or any other town in England. But in Ireland I'm turning into a soldier with every day that passes, he thought. His mind continued to wander towards that better time, which was only a few months ago, but might as well have been a hundred years past now.

Saturday September 11th 1920 started clear and calm with a beautiful sunny blue sky, it was a moderately warm early autumn day. Sgt. Collins stood looking out the top window of the barracks at the fantastic view of the sunny early morning and as he finished buttoning his green police tunic. What a lovely day for this time of year, he thought. He looked at the time on the clock – 6 a.m. Tyrone hadn't had a day like this in the summertime, and all it did was rain. I'm going to make the most of this day before winter arrives, he thought. He marched downstairs to inspect the constables who stood to attention in the public office; they were Constable Ignatius Foley from Co. Kerry, Constable Matthew Jennings from Co. Tipperary, Constable Jonathan Fennell from Co. Waterford and Constable Tobias Cullinan from Co. Wexford.

"Right men we are going out on cycle patrol this nice sunny day, get them ready for five minutes time and I will meet you at the front door." They all dashed off as quickly as they could to collect their equipment and transport. At the front door the men all glanced cheerfully at Sergeant Collins, and each other, as they mounted the bicycles, Collins smiled back. "Boys, it's a lovely day, I hope our work will be the same, I don't want any arrests unless we have to, the cell doors are empty and lying open in the barracks, and that's the way I want them to stay," he ordered.

"Yes Sgt." came the cheerful reply, "we will do our best."

"I'm glad to hear that," he replied. "I mean it, men, no arrests – we don't need the trouble or the paperwork." They all set off cycling through the village two by two, with Collins leading the way and waving at the passers-by as they went. Soon the policemen were cycling along the hedgerow lined-lanes of Ireland listening to the chirp of waking birds and getting distracted by the beautiful blue sky. They were all so glad to be taking this pleasant morning jaunt. "Right men, let's pick up the pace for a bit and see how fit we are," said Collins, they groaned back in the expected discomfort, but it was followed by a laugh.

"Foley you are not fit," smirked Fennell.

"Bollox to you, Fennell, I'll beat you any day in a race," said Foley as they all pedalled furiously, passing the farmland and soft green pastures of Ulster.

*

When the patrol came to a stop, Collins peered over the hedge and watched an elderly gentleman lifting bales of hay by himself onto a cart. There was a lot more hay for him to lift and he had only five or six on the horse cart. "Hello there," shouted Collins, "it's a nice day for work." The old man stared back, he was all bent over.

"Yes, it is a lovely day, I'm just getting the last of it in before the weather turns bad," he answered. Collins scratched his nose in bemusement.

"Have you nobody to help you?" he asked him.

"No, nobody, my wife will be down with food later, and that's all the help I'll get, but sure I'll be grand on my own," said the farmer.

Collins shook his head. "The speed you are going at you will be here to next week lifting that load," said Collins, "we will help you." He reached out his hand. "My name is Sergeant Patrick Collins and these are my men."

"I'm Ben Clancy, this is my land," said the old man. "Thanks for your help."

"That's what we're here for," Collins answered. "Let's get to work, boys, with the hay," he said. "It's a warm day so you can take your tunics off for this bit of work." The men were delighted to remove them.

"That is good news, Sgt.," said Constable Cullinan, "I'm sweating like a pig in my buttoned-up tunic." The men soon got to work on the hay, throwing in a human chain from the newly cut field of stubble, and soon it was piled high on the old man's red wooden cart, like bricklayers making a wall; they packed it all in tightly. Ben sat and watched the policeman as they got his work done for him. "You just sit there, Ben, we won't be long," said Collins, and in no time at all the hay was ready for the barn.

"Thank you, my wife will soon be down with the food, I'm hungry just watching you," he said.

"We might stay," said Foley, "but that is up to the Sgt."

"What kind of food is she bringing? I need something to drink; I'm thirsty," said Flaherty.

"The warm sun has brought out a thirst in us all." Before long, Ben's wife arrived with a big wicker basket.

"Good day gentlemen," she said, slightly shocked. "I didn't think my husband would have much done, but I'd like to thank you all for helping him. Will you stay for some food?"

"What do have, ma'am?" asked Jennings.

"Bread, newly baked, butter fresh from the churn, boiled eggs and ham, cold buttermilk and tea."

"Yes," said Collins, "we can stay for food." Everybody found a place to sit and relaxed in the sun as they enjoyed the bread, butter, boiled eggs, ham, and ice-cold buttermilk.

"Police work couldn't get any better than this, Sergeant Collins," said Constable Fennell.

Collins nodded. "Yes Fennell, today is going well, I hope it lasts, I really do. We will take a quick rest here before we continue on our patrol, and then we can go back to the village." The beautiful sunny morning turned to a lovely warm afternoon, and by the time the six-man police cycle patrol got back to Sixmilecross, it was a cool bright evening, as they turned on into the main street, the melodic sounds of a fiddle drifted in the evening air.

"What's going on?" said Flaherty.

"It's Sean Doherty from Donegal," said Collins, "he is the fiddler on the road, he moves from house to house and village to village all over Donegal, Tyrone, and Fermanagh. He is a gentleman of the road, truly, the past preserved. His father and grandfather did the same, he is also a tinsmith, you will see him walking the roads in his tidy grey suit and flat cap, his fiddle under one arm and his sheets of tin and a little canvas bag of work tools under the other. He is also a wonderful storyteller." The village had come out of their homes to hear him play, he looked up and saw the policemen get off their bicycles.

"Good evening to you gentlemen," he said, as he stopped playing.

"Good evening Mr Doherty, it's so nice to see you again," said Collins. "Please Sean, don't let me stop you playing."

"Grand," he said, "what tune do you want me to play?" Collins thought for a moment.

"Can you play me 'The Fox Chase'?"

"I will," he said, and with that he stamped his feet and started to play the wonderful tune.

"Stay here, men," Collins ordered, "I'm going to check up on the barracks. Flaherty you come with me." Both men walked towards the building. The music flowed like water, Sean played 'The Fox Chase' again, along with 'The Hare and the Hounds', 'The Flowers of Red Hill' and other pleasant-sounding jigs and reels of old Ireland. Collins threw open the front door of the barracks so the music could drift in, and Flaherty was on the front desk in the public office, the cell doors were open and empty just as Collins had wanted them to be. He went and stood in the front door and watched the happy party enjoy their happiness.

If only every day could be as good as September 11th 1920, he thought.

CHAPTER EIGHT

SIXMILECROSS, IRELAND

21ST NOVEMBER 1920

"Constable Jennings, what has happened to the train?" said Collins.

"I can tell you now, sir, I spoke to the station master," said Jennings. The four policemen stood on the platform next to the train as it waited in the station until the investigation was complete, the time was now 4 p.m. Steam hissed lightly from the sides of the great iron beast. Jennings looked down at his notebook and read from the information he had collected. "The goods/mail train was making its way to Sligo when at 12.20 p.m. four men armed with pistols entered the signal cabin here at Sixmilecross, they forced the signalman to set the signal to red. When the train came to a halt, twenty men appeared and held the train crew at gunpoint. They were made to kneel down on the platform and swear they wouldn't work on any trains containing munitions or military stores," Jennings continued. "The mail sorters were also held at gunpoint and the raiders seized letters addressed to

Police Headquarters in Omagh, Sligo, and Enniskillen. They also took letters marked on His Majesty's Service, the incident lasted an hour and the gunmen, according to two eyewitnesses, simply strolled out of the station in a leisurely fashion to their waiting motor cars and drove away. We recovered two mail bags which contained about 700 letters, postcards, and circulars. In the first bag the letters had been opened and marked with the inscription 'PCB–IRA' and in the second bag there are two sets of unopened letters addressed to every policeman in Sixmilecross Barracks." Collins bit his lip.

"Have you worked out what PCB–IRA means?"

Whelan spoke in a worried voice; "We think it means Passed by Censor – Irish Republican Army." Collins and his men tried not to think of how serious to them the situation was about to become.

"Alright Constable Jennings tell the station master that the train can travel on to Sligo now, we will bring these letters back to the men and open them in the barracks together at the same time." The men sat in the main room of the barracks, Collins stood in front of them with his two letters in his hand. They were not from the same people as the first one was a small, plain brown envelope with a Belfast postmark. "I will open this letter first," he said, he put his finger in the top of the envelope and ripped into it. On the page he could see a black skull and crossbones and the letter said, "There is not enough room in this world for me and you and one of us is going to leave it." Collins laughed and gave a sigh of relief, the rest of the men did the same. "It's still a threat that we will take seriously, boys," he said as he put the brown envelope on the table. He then took a deep breath and picked up the second letter, this one was different – it was in a medium-sized white, expensive-looking envelope with a Dublin postmark. "Let's see what we have in this letter" he said. "To whom it may concern, this is to inform you that any further collaboration with the forces of occupation will be punishable by death. You have been warned. Signed The Irish Republican Army." Collins looked at his men.

"Fuck me, boys, this is serious, I feel quite sick reading those words. This is the same letter that the G men in Dublin Castle got last week and most of them got shot dead in their beds all around the city this morning!" The men all sat in silence looking at their Sergeant, hoping he had the answer for what to do next. "Look lads it's up to you, I won't impose this on any man here, but from this moment on we have reached a point of no return. I will give you a few minutes to think about it, but there's the door, if you feel you can't go any further. I won't think any less of you for it."

Everybody sat and thought about the grave situation they were all in. Whelan put his hand up.

"Sir what do you plan to do?"

"What can I do? I'm forty-eight years old and I don't know any other job than this, I have no choice, I must carry on. I mean, who else is going to give me a job at my age? And anyway, I'm a widower with seven grown up children. I have nothing to lose, so I'm staying here and that's it!"

Constable Foley stood up. "I haven't seen my wife in months or my five children, this letter is the final straw. I'm resigning from the force, after all I'm a policeman, not a soldier. I'm going to pack my clothes and personal effects now, I will write my resignation letter and leave it with you, Sergeant." Foley took off his tunic, placed it on the desk, and went upstairs to change out of his uniform. The rest of the men decided to stay with the Sergeant rather than leave the RIC. Foley came down the stairs in his civilian suit carrying a battered brown suitcase. "Gentlemen I'm sorry but it is not worth the risk for a few pounds anymore, I'm sorry but good luck and god bless you all." With those words Foley walked out of the barracks and down the main street of the village to the railway station on his way to catch the next train to Dublin. The phone rings and Collins answers it, it is RIC Headquarters in Dublin at Phoenix Park. He listens in silence to the news.

"Yes sir, thank you, I will pass the message on. Right men," he said, "that was Headquarters on the phone, a day that has started badly has just got worse and worse. That raid on the football match by the police and military at Croke Park has left fourteen people dead. It's being called Bloody Sunday, we have been ordered to get out the barbed wire and the sandbags from the store room and put them in the windows of the barracks and expect an attack at any time from the IRA. I'm also suspending the foot patrols on main street until further notice. I will do the patrols alone, and have your rifles at the ready, they are not to go in the gun rack until I say." The men get straight to their duties that they were ordered to do. Then within a few minutes another telephone call from Dublin Castle confirms the deaths at the football match at Croke Park. Collins goes into his office to complete his nightly reports to Phoenix Park and Dublin Castle. It had been a momentous day. Sgt. Collins comes back into the room and says, "I will ask you all again, if any man wants to join ex Constable Foley and leave then there is the door."

Whelan spoke up; "We're all staying. What about you, Sgt. have you changed your mind?"

"No," said Collins, "I will not be intimidated by anybody. I'm staying to see it through and that's my decision, I'm not for turning."

CHAPTER NINE

SIXMILECROSS, IRELAND

SUNDAY 28TH NOVEMBER 1920

The following Sunday the barracks waited for the expected attack by the IRA, but it had not yet materialized. Anyhow, right at this moment, Collins and his men had more pressing police matters to attend with, as today was the last horse and cattle fair of the year in Tyrone. Thousands of people would descend on the village by train, cart, motor car, and on foot.

"Jennings, have we enough men to police today's fair?" asked Collins.

"No sir," said Jennings.

"Grand, then it's good I rang headquarters in Omagh requesting more constables. They are coming from Omagh, Strabane, and Dungannon on the train at 12 p.m., the fair won't start until 2 p.m. so we will have men in place and be ready for what might happen." The telephone rings, Collins answers it, the time is 9 a.m. He listens to every detail from the caller for a few minutes.

"Thank you sir for ringing, with the description you have just provided me with, it seems as if it's my old nemesis, and he's back and up to his old tricks again." He put the phone down quickly. "Constable Whelan, I need you to come with me now, that phone caller has claimed that he has been beaten up by somebody in the village and I believe I know who." They get up and Collins fixes his tunic button then both men go outside to where the alleged assault took place, outside O'Leary's public house.

"What happened to you, sir?" said Whelan. A small man stood beside the pub, he had a badly swollen face.

"I got punched by Alexander Jackson, he hit me around the face a few times and I fell down," said the man.

"What is your name?" said Whelan.

"Sean Murphy, I was working behind the bar last night and I refused to serve him drink. I was going for a walk before mass and he just came over and punched me."

"Right," said Collins. "We will find him and arrest him, come into the barracks later and make a complaint. We'll look for him now, he can't have gone too far." The two policemen start searching the village for him.

"So who is Alexander Jackson?" asked Whelan. Collins took his cap off and scratched his head.

"Alexander Jackson, or Alec as he is known, is my greatest headache. I have arrested him more times but he just doesn't learn, or care, his life is full of badness and crime, he served in the Royal Navy from 1916 to 1918 at Scappa Flow during the great war. He has two tattoos on his hand, a ship's anchor and a palm tree, he also fought as a boxer on the ship, his criminal record goes back to 1913 and 1914 for larceny, which were both discharged, then two counts of larceny in 1915, again discharged. In 1919 he was fined 10 shillings for assault then later that year he got probation for assault and robbery. He is only out of prison this year as he got jailed for two months in Crumlin Road prison for yet another assault and robbery, plus he was fined forty shillings for riotous behaviour, then another forty shillings for breaking a curfew, a truly nasty man," said Collins.

No sooner had Collins stopped telling the stories of Alec when Collins spies him. Whelan is totally surprised to see a rather smartly dressed man instead of the monster he was expecting. Jackson stood in an arrogant fashion in front of the two policemen; he wore a smart pin stripped suit and grey fedora hat which was cocked slightly to the side. He looked like a Chicago gangster. He just grins at them, his sharp youthful face lights up on seeing the Sergeant.

"Ahh Sergeant Collins we meet again." He reaches down to clean his bright shiny boots. "I hate wearing boots, I'd rather wear my spatts but it's too dirty to walk around the village in that kind of footwear."

Collins barked at him, "Did you punch Sean Murphy this morning?" Alex just stared back at the two policemen.

"Yes, I hit him," he said.

"Right Alex, you are under arrest, you need to come with us."

"Alright I will come quietly, you don't need any handcuffs, I won't run away." Jackson shrugs his shoulders and walks calmly down the street to the barracks with the two men. Collins locked him in his cell, the big heavy keys clanked loudly as he shut the door behind him.

"He will stay there until Monday morning when he goes to court."

"More fucking paperwork for this bloody nuisance," says Collins angrily. "And this horse fair, I could do without all this shit today, but first we have got to go to mass and every man should be unarmed going to church. Constable Fennell you will stay here and take charge of the station, the rest of you can follow me to mass." The policemen put on their heavy green coats and walked in single file down to the village chapel for mass.

Father John McChesney stood with his arms out stretched in prayer, he was a young handsome priest with neat, black hair parted at the side, aged around thirty-five. He smiled at the congregation as he spoke the Latin mass; *"Deaus, deaus meaus: quare tristis es anima mea, et quare contrubas me."* The congregation all bowed their heads in prayer. Father McChesney continued the Latin mass and Sgt. Collins and his men sat at the front of the church praying in silence. He bent over the host and said, *"Hoc est enim corpus meum."* The bell was rung and they all bowed their heads again. At the end of the mass Father McChesney gave his final words of the sermon; *"Ite missa est."*

Collins and his men answered, *"Deo gratias"* which meant in English 'thanks be to God'. He then addressed his flock in English;

"Before we go home, I would like to thank the Sergeant, Patrick Collins, and the men of the Royal Irish Constabulary who paid for the new high alter that we have today. So before we go could we have a round of applause for them." The congregation clapped their hands politely for what the policemen had done for the church. As the noise of the applause rippled loudly around the church Sgt. Collins was pleased. "And we all pray for a nice quiet day at the fair also," said Father McChesney sternly.

After mass, Collins called his men into the public office of the barracks. "I have just taken two phone calls in the last few minutes, County Inspector O'Callahan called to say there will not be the numbers of policemen that we expected to help us, so there will be less of us for the fair, and Lord Copeland called to offer his Special Constables to assist us but I turned them down. A few things to point out: keep an eye out for pickpockets as there will be teams of them mingling in the crowd, also we will try and not make too many arrests for public order offences, we have only the four cells in the barracks. So I'd say a few whacks of the truncheon might be enough, the other thing is the IRA used the fair to attack Drumquin Barracks in August to steal our guns, so be on your guard for another attack from them. Right men, check we have the equipment we need today, handcuffs, truncheon, whistle, and your pistols. I don't want any man carrying a rifle, now let's get outside and get to work." Under a cold grey midday sun Collins and his men marched down the village street. "We are going to take up positions in twos, I will make my way down to the railway station to meet our reinforcements for today's fair. Whelan come with me, the rest of you take up your posts." The 12 o'clock train arrived on time and whatever extra policemen the RIC could send to Sixmilecross got out of the carriages and stood to attention on the platform waiting for the local Sergeant to take charge.

"Men you know the drill and what is expected

today, keep an eye out for pickpockets and trouble makers but try not to make too many arrests as the cells are not big enough to hold too many people, just give them a good hard wallop with your truncheons and that should sort it out. Now follow me please." Collins made his way back towards the village with his green-coated followers behind him.

The policemen stood in twos at strategic points all around the village, ready for the expected crowd to start arriving, and soon enough the small village street began to fill up with small men, big men, some fat, some thin, others were tall, men with walking sticks, all wearing suits with flat caps and the men with more money wore black bowler hats. Horses were paraded to the buying public up and down the street, steel hooves on cobblestones echoed noisily and tobacco smoke filled the air. Pigs were kept in wire cages, ready to be sold for a few pounds or shillings and a crescendo of male voices got louder and louder as great gallons of porter and stout were sold and drank in the public houses. Collins and Whelan left their position at the corner of the street and began to walk through the vast crowd, they were showing everyone at the fair that the police were there and in force should trouble arrive.

CHAPTER TEN

SIXMILECROSS, IRELAND

28TH NOVEMBER 1920

"Calm down, calm down," Collins grabbed a man who was throwing punches at everybody that stood too close to him and wrestled him to the ground. Darkness had descended in more ways than one. "If you don't calm down, you're going to the barracks, ya drunken bollox." More constables arrived to assist Collins, Whelan had the man by the coat lapels. "Right boys, take this gobshite to the barracks, I'm not putting up with this behaviour any longer." He is taken by the scruff of his unwashed neck by two constables and marched off to the jail cell.

Further up the street, another fight had broken out. "You bastard you owe me money for a drink!" Two men were punching each other's faces and a crowd had gathered to watch the boxing match. Collins glanced at his watch; it was 11 p.m. He landed his truncheon on one of the men's shoulders with a thud. "Stop fighting now," he roared. The two men didn't take any notice, instead they continued landing more blows on each other. It takes four constables using their truncheons to calm things down, but just as it looked like the police were getting things under control another big fight starts, the shrill sounds of the constables' whistles filled the night, calling for more assistance to another disturbance somewhere else in the village. Collins has had enough of clearing out the fighting mobs of drunken men.

"I'm ordering my men to close the pubs now, that's it, the fair is long over and it's time to get this under control." He ordered some of his constables to close every public house in the village and ordered the rest of them to push the mob up towards the railway station. "Men use your truncheons, let's get these bastards onto the last train and out of the village." Very soon the thinnest of green lines swept the mob towards the open doors of the carriages. "All of you get to fuck in the train and go to sleep, the fair is over, and your fighting is finished too." These words seemed to work as the mob turned quiet again and boarded the train, as the train pulled out of the station most of the men had fallen asleep.

"It's a miracle," said Whelan.

"Well if it's a miracle it's a lump-of-brown-wood-with-some-guts-behind-it-miracle" answered Collins. The train and its now sleeping drunken passengers and the constables who had been drafted in from other areas also boarded the train, they were all soon on their way from the village and peace was restored once again. Collins and his men walked back to the barracks, he had his nightly paperwork reports to write up for RIC HQ in Dublin and Dublin Castle. The news from the Constable on the desk was like last Sunday, grim! First Collins ordered that Alexander Jackson and the man caught fighting at the fair be released. "Sean Murphy has said he does not want to press charges against Jackson, and the bollox that was drunk and fighting can make his own way home." The constable again spoke of the bad news from County Cork.

"Sgt., more bad news, a party of the RIC Auxiliary Division was travelling on a raid or patrol from their headquarters in Macroom Castle to Dunmanway when they were ambushed at Kilmichael, all seventeen were killed." Collins shook his head.

"When did this happen?"

"Sometime this afternoon sir, the Crossley lorry was burned and now as we speak they are still lying on the road. Everyone is too frightened to go and remove their dead bodies in case the Rebels Flying Column is still in the area waiting to attack again." This was escalation in the IRA's guerrilla campaign.

To be able to attack men of an elite division, who had seen fighting in the great war, and kill every one of them was a shock, and for the police and military to leave the bodies at the roadside over night was more proof of how dangerous the situation was getting in Ireland.

The war was getting closer to Sixmilecross Barracks and it was surely now only a matter of time before the trouble arrived.

CHAPTER ELEVEN

The men sat in the barracks drinking tea. "Where is Sgt. Collins?" asked Whelan.

"He is out alone doing a foot patrol on the main street," said Fennell. "He's mad, always wanting to walk the main street every time he is on duty, as if the people in the village give a fuck!" The men laughed. "Did you know he has a nickname, boys?" said Fennell.

"What is it?" asked Whelan.

"He is called the Green Fella."

"Why is he called that?" enquired Whelan.

"It is because his name is Collins and he is from Cork, people suggest that he is related to Michael Collins."

"What a load of rubbish, calling him that," said Whelan. Jennings changed the subject, he knew the Sergeant was out doing a beat patrol of the village and might come back early just in time to catch the conversation.

"Lads it's five minutes past midnight, Happy New Year boys."

"Happy New Year 1921 goodbye 1920, I hope the new year will be a better one," said Jennings. The front door opened and Collins walked in.

"Happy New Year sir," said Whelan.

"Thanks boys, but it could be worse than last year," said Collins coldly. "I need a big mug of hot tea, it's very cold out there, another dark dreary New Year's Day." The men went quiet and their mood darkened slightly. 1920 was not an easy year and the thought of the new year becoming worse wasn't a good prospect. Collins took the mug of tea and walked towards the warm fire in the public office; he took the patrol book and added his entry for his beat on the street that he just completed.

"Constable Fennell, I want you to telephone Omagh and wish Inspector O'Callahan a Happy New Year."

"Yes sir," he replied. Jennings picked up the telephone to make the call. "Sir the lines is dead." Collins ran to the phone and placed it to his ear.

"Oh no, men get your rifles, now! We're about to be attacked, the telephone wires have been cut, get the fucking rifles!" A bullet whined in, smashing the main barrack's window and shattered glass all over the men. The hot shard of metal blew right through Constable Jennings' chest in a spray of bone matter and blood that spattered the furniture and wall of the public office in a bright crimson arch. Jennings was lifted off his feet by the impact and it slammed him down on to the rough wooden floor, then the sound of the gunshot caught with the bullet ringing through the street and the building. The other constables dived for cover. Shouts of obscenities and screams of surprise echoed from the barracks. Jennings groaned, "I'm hit, I'm hit!" Blood was pouring from his wound, his strength draining from his body as his life was ebbing away. Jennings spoke no more; he had died in a sea of his own blood. The policemen lay on the floor as bullets whizzed and wined through the walls and the now broken windows, the barracks was under attack by a large party of around thirty men in an IRA Flying Column. It was hard to return fire so, for the moment, the men lay on the floor next to Jennings' lifeless blood-covered body as the volleys of shots continued to rain down on them. Fennell looked at Collins with frightened eyes.

"We're all going to get killed here," he said.

"No we're not, just stay low for now and get behind the heavy wooden desk," ordered Collins. "Whelan," he roared, "get the Varey gun, we need to get a flare up to alert the military in Omagh that were under attack."

"Yes sir, I'll try once the shooting dies down a bit." Collins raised his rifle, he could make out a man standing in a raincoat and soft cap firing at the edge of the shop wall on the other side of the road. Collins fired off a few well-aimed shots and the man dropped down, splashed in blood.

Whelan scrambled along the floor with the flare gun towards the back door, the bullets were still popping and rattling through the police building. The attack was at the front of the building so hopefully nobody was attacking the back of the building, but it would still be dangerous to open the back door. Whelan opened the door gently, put his arm out, and shot the flare skywards. He then shut the door quickly and dived down on the floor. The flare shot upwards in the night sky and exploded in a bright reddish white light, it hung in the air and lit up the village and the surrounding countryside. The military would see the flare in Omagh and they would be here with reinforcements soon. Outside the sounds of a Crossley tender could be heard over the noise of the rifle fire, it stopped and the men of Lord Copeland's Special Constabulary appeared in their Crossley 'Roaring Meg'. It was a welcome sound for the men lying on the floor of the building. They had arrived to engage the Flying Column, the firing on the barracks stopped and another gun battle started but the policemen in the barracks still stayed lying on the floor, waiting for the column to leave. The roar of a heavy military lorry could be heard in the distance, this was the signal for the IRA to leave the area – they were now outgunned and outnumbered. They made off across the fields as quickly as they could. The Specials and the soldiers arrived at the barracks. Lord Copeland was the first to walk through the shattered barrack door.

"Is anybody hurt, Sgt Collins?" he asked.

"Yes, Constable Jennings has been killed," he answered.

"That's awful news," said Lord Copeland. "Any rebels hit?"

"Yes, I hit one man for sure," said Collins. Lord Copeland pointed to one of his Special Constables. "Get your men to check the area, Collins shot one of the rebels." The Specials did a sweep of the village.

"Sir we found a large pool of blood across the road, he did shoot one of them but the body or person has been taken away."

"Alright boys, thanks, keep looking." A smartly dressed Army officer was the next man to walk through the door.

"Allow me to introduce myself, my name is

Captain Rupert Cavendish Jones of the 1st Battalion Yorkshire Regiment." He spoke with a posh and plummy English accent. "So sorry to hear you lost a man tonight, Sgt." Collins nodded in appreciation. He reached out his hand.

"I'm Sergeant Patrick Joseph Collins RIC."

"Delighted to meet you, old boy," said the Captain.

"Lord Copeland, thank you for coming to help us."

"Sgt. you know we are here to help you, it is a good job that we didn't listen to your superior officers or some of those idiots in Dublin Castle about supplying us with whistles and caps for summoning the RIC, as we have seen tonight that idea was sheer folly." Collins said nothing, only to thank him and his men again. Lord Copeland spoke to Captain Rupert. "Captain, would you and your men like to join me and my Special Constables for a glass of sherry at my house to toast the new year, I'd ask Sgt. Collins to join us but he has a bit of tidying up to do."

"Sounds like a good idea," said the Captain. Collins wasn't pleased with that remark and Lord Copeland had noticed. "I'm very sorry about the death of Constable Jennings, please convey my condolences to his family."

"Thank you, sir, I will," said Collins. The lord and the captain left the building for the warmth of Lord Copeland's stately home, leaving the Sergeant and his

Constables to clean up.

*

A few days after the murder, the body of Constable Jennings was taken to the railway station in a rough wooden coffin. He was to be taken to Tipperary to be interred in his native county. When the coffin was safely on board the train, a man got off in a smart suit from the front carriage. His name was Constable Donal Sheehan from Galway, he was Constable Jennings replacement.

CHAPTER TWELVE

SIXMILECROSS, IRELAND

FEBRUARY 1921

Moonlight bathed and washed Collins, his men, and the Tyrone countryside in a cold but soothing ivory. The quiet February night was broken by the sounds of a questioning owl as the ten policemen travelled on their bicycles to a country lane a few miles outside the village. Bicycle patrols have been found most useful, especially at night where quietness is needed; a motor vehicle would be no use in a house raid because the noise of the car would give the patrol away. Collins cycled at the front, all the men were in single file. "Don't forget men, that no civilian, cyclist, or motor car is allowed to pass us, we don't want any information being giving on the approach of our patrol," he said. Collins was proud of his small band of men as they moved cautiously along the dirt road.

"Boys, can we stop for a rest under those trees in the distance?" asked Fennell, Collins agreed.

"Yes, why not," he said. When they got to the

trees the men got off their mounts. "We will shelter here for a few minutes out of the cold," said Collins.

"I'd light a fire if I could," joked Whelan. The mood turned serious.

"What is this thing called partition, sir?" asked Constable Sheehan.

"I don't really know much about it myself so I can't say what will happen but I don't think now is the time to be talking about politics," said Collins. "I just don't trust politicians of any type," he said.

After a few minutes the men remounted their bicycles only to be met with a volley of shots from a group of gunmen wearing long trench coats and flat caps that were hiding on a nearby hillside. Constable Flaherty took a direct hit to the head; a bullet smashed into his right ear, travelled through his brain, and sent him tumbling to the ground. The rest of the policemen went running and screaming in terror towards the safety of a grass bank near the trees, leaving their bicycles abandoned on the road next to the injured Flaherty. They crawled on their hands and knees behind the bank, fumbling to get their rifles ready. Collins scrambled towards them with his gun primed to return fire. The IRA had been keeping this particular stretch of road under observation from a hillside 400 yards away, waiting for an opportunity to attack a passing patrol. Unfortunately for Collins and his men, the police sheltering under the trees presented a prime target. Constable Flaherty's lifeless body lay in a large red lake of his own blood. A pitter patter of bullets spluttered and danced at the front of the bank where the policemen cowered in fear, throwing up the earth in small neat brown clouds.

"Try and return fire," said Cullinan, he leaned over the bank and fired his rifle at the attackers but a bullet caught him in the neck, spraying the other men in an eruption of crimson blood. He groaned, gargled, and slumped down behind the bank and didn't move again. The rapid-fire bullet storm from the IRA Flying Column continued towards the policemen, behind the protection of the mound of earth, chewing up the ground once more and spitting mud up in the air.

"Maybe the bastards will run out of ammunition," said Whelan.

"I fucking hope so," said Collins. "It's the only way we'll get out of here alive." The patrol all leaned forward and began returning accurate fire towards the attackers on the hillside; smoke and fire belched from the policemen's Lee Enfield rifles in a rapid-fire response, hitting two of the gunmen in a spray of blood. Very soon thereafter, the firing from the hillside stopped. After waiting for a few minutes, Collins, seizing the moment, let a wild cry out of him. "Make a run for that shooting position." Everybody was frightened but they still jumped up from their places of safety and ran towards the gunmen.

When they got to the spot, the IRA had fled and left, leaving a large pool of fresh blood behind. Whelan was first to reach the area.

"Look Sergeant there is blood on the ground along with tea and some food." Collins stared at the ground.

"We have at least killed or wounded some of them, they must have been waiting for quite some time to have tea and food here," he said. "There is not much we can do now, the rebels have gone now, let's get back to the bicycles again." Constable Flaherty and Cullinan were both dead, the rest of the men stood next to the bodies.

"How will we get back to the barracks?" asked Sheehan, then the sounds of a lorry driving up the road in the direction towards them sent the nervous men running for the bank. Collins, however, didn't run, he stood in the middle of the road waiting for the lorry. "Stop, stop," he ordered. The lorry halted, a dirtied face peered from the driver's window, he looked scared.

"Can I help you Sergeant?" he remarked.

"Can you take us back to Sixmilecross? My men have been shot up and two have been killed."

"Yes of course I can help, just climb on the back and I will drive you to the village," said the lorry driver. They all clambered onto the back of the open truck, lifting their two dead comrades and the bicycles onto the bare wooden boards and sat holding on as best they could, ready for the sombre drive back to the barracks. Constable Flaherty and Constable Cullinan's bodies were brought through the main doors and placed in the back room.

"Whelan get some sand, put it down on the corridor and in the rooms to soak up the blood," said Collins. "It's been a tough evening."

CHAPTER THIRTEEN

SIXMILECROSS, IRELAND

MARCH 1921, 2.30 P.M.

March was cold and dry, and morning had turned into afternoon, the shadows that the two Crossley tenders threw across the Irish countryside changed direction as the motor cars skimmed along the lanes. It is 2.30 p.m., Sergeant Collins is leading the two tenders to patrol Aghnaglea Road just outside the village. "You all know, men, that it's just us today on patrol," said Collins, shouting to be heard over the noise of the motor vehicle engine. "The military and the Special Constabulary are conducting operations on the Derry/Tyrone border so if we get attacked today we will have no reinforcements to help." The men never said a word, they were used to being left to fend for themselves. The force was now stretched to breaking point.

"Sgt. Collins is it true that the RIC have been burned out of barracks all over Cork, Kerry, and beyond?" asked Whelan.

"Yes," he answered. "No proper reinforcements for the RIC have been available from when this trouble started a few years ago in 1919, we are scattered in small barracks with parties of six to eight constables all over Ireland. As you know, with our own situation in Sixmilecross, a lot of those isolated rural barracks have been attacked and burned and the men killed or captured, once that happened the other barracks were evacuated for tactical reasons which has been disastrous, then the IRA will go and burn them down. Police moral is at an all-time low and I'm still waiting for replacements for Constable Flaherty and Cullinan."

Sadly, what Collins was saying was all true, no reinforcements for the RIC were available in the winter of 1919-1920 and beyond, barracks were closed, and the police had lost control of whole areas. Also, constables, sergeants, and inspectors were constantly being moved and thus lost touch with the countryside, and the feeling of the inhabitants was lost to a great extent. Police 'intelligence' had suffered. These evacuations only raised the morale and prestige of Sinn Fein at the expense of the RIC. Sinn Fein took advantage of the situation and the burning of vacated barracks became a popular and safe amusement. The Crossleys continued along the Aghnaglea Road up towards the brow of the hill which they would turn right onto the Drumlester Road.

As they reached halfway up the hill, gunfire

poured down on them in a hellish hailstorm, the Flying Column was waiting for them behind the trees at the top of the road.

"Find some cover," Collins shouted to the men. They scrambled over the side of the motor car and took cover in the hedgerow growing on both sides of the road. The Flying Column stooped, shooting at the motor cars and directed fire on the men hiding in the hedgerow. Luckily for them the earth bank made excellent protection from the shooting. "Men lie down and don't get up, let them use up their ammunition on the mud, I'm sick of seeing my men getting killed, just stay down until I say so, don't return fire yet." The constables all lay with their rifles waiting for the command. The bullets continued to impact on the trees, chewing up the wood into tiny splinters and spitting the small brown fragments all over the men, lying prone on the ground doing no serious damage to their flesh or bones. Collins tactic of staying low and staying out of the way was working.

As yet more bullets pinged from the firing position at the top of the hill, the two Crossleys were undamaged, and the policemen hiding in fear stayed untouched. Collins knelt up and fired a round of shots back at his attackers then the rest of the men joined him in returning fire, keeping the IRA men pinned down, now it was their turn to be under attack from a hail of steel rain.

"Train the Lewis gun on the bastards," shouted Collins. The machine gun buzzed and spattered bullets in the direction of the IRA men who lay flat on their stomachs, trying to avoid the stuttering death that awaited the man who put his head up above the muddy parapet. The Lewis gun rounds hammered the bank, ricocheting and bringing death pounding at the door of the enemy, the battle raged on and a smell of cordite hung in the still air. Collins and his men stopped firing and hid again behind the muddy wall and the shooting on all sides stopped.

"It must be the first time in the history of war that nobody got shot, we were bloody lucky today," said Collins. The Flying Column retreated and left the hillside to silence again, they had run out of ammunition. Collins wasn't waiting to find out if they were coming back. "Everyone get into the Crossleys, NOW! Wer'e getting out of here fast," he barked. The men all climbed into the cars and drove noisily and quickly away towards Sixmilecross

Whelan and Collins stood behind the desk of the public office in the barracks; the rest of the policemen had gone for a cup of tea in the back room, two men in uniform walked through the door.

"My name is Constable Daithi McConnell from Limerick," said the first man.

"And my name is Constable Peader O'Dwyer

from Kilkenny," said the second. They were the replacements for the two constables killed in February.

"My name is Sergeant Patrick Joseph Collins and this is Constable Liam Whelan, welcome to Tyrone. I will brief you on what I expect of you and what the situation is here in the count," he added. He looked at Whelan, "Constable Whelan show these men to their quarters."

"Yes sir," he said and opened the door into the corridor, bringing the men towards the stairs and then Collins went and locked the front door of the barracks. That should not have been left open, he thought as he locked the door. The men all assembled in the back room waiting for their orders, smartly turned out again in clean uniforms. "Before we start I'd like to welcome our two new constables who have just arrived, Constable McConnell from Limerick and Constable O'Dwyer from Kilkenny. Men I think at the moment we are losing this war, the IRA Flying Columns are all over Ulster and they are winning, they are trying to force us out of the smaller barracks like the one we are in now and it's a ploy that has been working in other parts of Ireland. There is a rumour that Dan Breen, the man who shot two constables dead in Tipperary, is in Tyrone, but more likely he is in Belfast." An explosion ends the sergeant's meeting as a hand grenade hits the front wall, tearing a hole in the stone work and smashing the window glass, throwing everything up in a cloud of flame, fire, and fragments. "Aggh not again!" shouts Collins. "Get down on the floor." The new man McConnell goes to get his rifle, but Whelan stops him.

"Get down on the ground, that's the Flying Column again." As he peers out the door, he can see the attackers outside. "There is about twenty men driving up and down the village in a Charabang shooting on the barracks, we don't have enough men to take them on, let them shoot until their guns are out of bullets and they soon leave." They pulled up outside of the building and began blasting the walls again, muzzle bursts punched more holes in the building, hurtling debris all over the road and footpath.

The policemen all huddled on the floor. "These bastards are getting more brazen with every attack; it's bright day light and they can come without any worry and shoot the place up," said Collins.

The rifles continued rattling, slamming more lead into the barrack window raking the inside walls with bullet after bullet, covering the men in bits of white plaster falling like snow from the rafters. The Flying Column, proud of the work they had done, left the village grinning like happy schoolchildren on a day trip to the beach. Once the danger was over the men got up and checked the damage and thankfully nobody was injured in the shooting. "That was two attacks today men and nobody got hurt, but it won't always work out so well."

The building was badly damaged in the attack. Constable Fennell takes off his tunic and leaves it on the dusty table in the public office, and then he places his cap next to it. "That's it, Sergeant, I cannot do this job any longer, this last attack was the final straw. I have a wife and seven children at home in Waterford, it's not worth getting killed for. I resign from the RIC, from this moment onwards I'm not a policeman." He walks towards the stairs and goes up to change into his suit. A few minutes later he comes down, now out of his uniform. "I'm sorry Sergeant, I'm sorry boys but I just can't live and work like this anymore. See you again boys, and take care." Fennell walks out the door and makes his way in the direction of the train station. Collins doesn't speak; he just leaves the rest of the men standing in the public office and goes into his office.

"It's more paperwork for RIC HQ in Dublin and Dublin Castle," he says to himself as he walks into his room.

APRIL 1921

Sergeant Collins stared down at the letter he had received, from RIC Headquarters Dublin Castle dated March 27th, 1921.

To Sergeant Patrick Joseph Collins you have been awarded the King's Police Medal for Gallantry. You will be awarded your medal at a special ceremony in Dublin Castle 8th of April 1921 GOD SAVE THE KING.

*

It is 9 a.m. on an April morning. Sergeant Collins is standing at Belfast railway station, he is waiting to board the train for Dublin to receive the King's Police Medal for Gallantry. Beside the platform was the steam train ready to transport him to Dublin. The weather was cold and dry. Collins turned up the collar on his warm woolen great coat, he was glad to be wearing it this morning. Collins climbed into the carriage and sat down on his seat, he had the carriage all to himself. He opened a newspaper which was left for him to read personally, it's so nice to get VIP treatment for once, he thought. Sergeant Collins had earned it with his bravery last month when his patrol came under attack, the train pulled slowly forward out of the station and Sergeant Collins settled in to read his newspaper. The train moved slowly from the station out of the city and into lush green fields. Sergeant Collins glanced out the window, the train was travelling through open countryside, the grim city of Belfast was a long way back in the distance, the city of Dublin would be soon fast approaching. As the train continued through the Irish countryside, Collins put his newspaper down and decided to have a sleep, he put his head back on the carriage seat, closed his eyes, and began to drift off. A knock on the carriage door soon told him that Dublin City was a few minutes away. He been asleep for most of the journey. Now he was in Dublin. Collins stepped down from the train onto the busy platform, he began to walk along it towards the exit of the station A car was waiting to take him to Dublin Castle for the medal presentation.

Later, Collins is back on board the train bound to Belfast. There was no big fuss about receiving his medal, no big speeches, just thank you for your service and back to work. He wasn't even wearing the medal, Dublin was too dangerous a place for showing off your wears, he just got back on the train and back to Belfast and on to Tyrone for more murder and mayhem.

CHAPTER FOURTEEN

SIXMILECROSS, IRELAND

MAY 1921

Sgt. Collins stood in the public office in his smart clean suit and put his grey flat cap on his head. It was his day off and he planned to go away for the day, alone.

"Constable Whelan I'm leaving you in charge of everything until I come back."

"Yes sir," said Whelan. "Where do you plan to go to, sir? so we know where you are."

"Nowhere special, Whelan, I'm taking the train to Omagh, I just need a few hours to myself to have a bit of a walk and clear my head."

"Right you are, sir, enjoy your day. I will be here at my post when you get back." Collins walked out the door into the warm afternoon sun and took the short walk to the railway station. Sitting on the train as it clanked its way to Omagh he stared out the window at the hedgerow-hemmed fields rolling past his window. He hadn't actually told Whelan the full story, only half of it. He was planning to meet inspector O'Callahan for afternoon tea. His thoughts turned to Cork and how he was still hopeful of a transfer to his native county.

"It's good to see you," said O'Callahan as they shook hands with each other in Omagh station. "We will go to my favourite tearoom in the main street of the town," said O'Callahan as both men walked away together for their well-earned refreshments.

Collins sipped his tea first, then nibbled his scone, trying not to get any strawberry jam on his jacket. He looked at O'Callahan sitting opposite. "What are the chances of getting my transfer to an RIC barracks in Cork soon, Inspector?" he asked. O'Callahan took a drink then put the cup down as he swallowed the tea.

"I don't think it looks good for your move for a lot of different reasons, firstly the IRA has almost taken over that part of the country, and they have burned down barracks, killed policemen and made it ungovernable, the other reason is the politicians have been working on deals behind everyone's backs. Collins, you know what partition is?" asked O'Callahan.

"Yes I have heard of it but I don't think it will happen, I mean it's unworkable, it will fall apart!"

O'Callahan scolded him, "Sergeant Collins, please don't be so naïve, I've been following everything that has been happening on the subject. On the 25th of

February 1920 the government of Ireland bill was introduced before parliament in London and it proposed two Irish parliaments, one in Belfast and one in Dublin. It was then given royal assent on the 23rd of December 1920 and it came into law on the 1st of May 1921 this year, so mark my words it will happen."

"So what, what will happen to us in the RIC?" asked Collins.

"That I don't know," said O'Callahan. "But you can bet it won't be good when the politicians are doing their dirty deals as usual."

"I don't like politicians regardless if they are orange, green, Tory, or liberal," said Collins. "They can never be trusted, never trust a politician, that's what I think."

"If there is a peace agreement, I think we will be the sacrificial lambs for the slaughter," said the Inspector, "but this conversation goes no further."

Collins stared into his cup quietly; the enormity of his situation was dawning on him. "It looks like I'm stuck between a rock and a hard place, but what can I do? The situation is out of my control," he said.

"What do you plan to do, Sergeant Collins?" said O'Callahan.

"There isn't a lot that I cannot do, there is no point in worrying, I'm just going to have to tough it out."

Collins finished his tea and stood up. "I think I will go for a walk around the town, would you like to join me?"

"No thanks, you go on, I'm going to sit here and take it easy." Collins reached over and shook O'Callahan's hand.

"I will meet you again, sir, take care and goodbye." Collins strides out of the tearoom, if he was worried about his situation, he wasn't showing it.

*

The walk around Omagh on this beautiful day was quite a pleasant experience for Collins, it was good to get away from the stress of Sixmilecross Barracks and the police work. He walked slowly down George Street, right past the courthouse that he was so used to visiting and onto the high street. He looked in the brightly coloured shop windows at the wares this small market town had to offer. Once he reached the bottom of Market Street, he decided to turn and go back up the town again. "I could do with a pint of stout while I wait for my train back to the village, I don't drink alcohol very often so one drink won't hurt." He soon found a pub on the high street and walked in, there were a number of people sitting at the bar, so he walked over and ordered a pint of creamy black stout and sat down. A small thin man sat and watched Collins at the bar as if he recognized him from somewhere.

"It's a lovely day," said Collins, trying to make conversation with the barman.

"I haven't seen much of it in here," replied the barman. Collins smiled and sat in silence. He found a newspaper to read and buried himself in the stories on the pages. The peace and quiet of the pub was soon disturbed by a man who walked in and everybody in the pub looked frightened of the new patron. "I'm sorry sir, I can't serve you," said the barman in a fearful voice.

"Why not?" asked the man sharply. Collins put down his newspaper, he recognized that voice, in an instant both men's eyes met across the bar. "Sgt. Collins, we meet again, the last time I was wearing my boots instead of my spats, today I have my spatts on. The Omagh roads are a lot cleaner than the dirt tracks of Sixmilecross," laughed Alexander Jackson as he pointed his finger at Collins. "Everybody, this is my good friend Sgt. Collins from Cork, hmm, that name sounds familiar, Collins from Cork."

"What do you mean by that?" the Sgt. Asked.

"Oh come on now, Patrick, you must be related to the Big Fella Michael Collins," he joked, "and, by the way, do you actually know that you also have a nickname, Patrick?"

"And just what is that, Alex?" he asked, his mood

turning angrier by the minute.

"Well you know that Mick Collins is the Big Fella and because you are related to him you are the Green Fella," Alex says, laughing. Sgt. Collins was red with rage.

"He is no relation of mine, whoever started this rumour is telling lies, it's nonsense!" Collins takes off his jacket.

"Don't you square up to me, Patrick," said Alex.

"Well you may not know but I've done a bit of boxing myself." said Sgt. Collins. Both men started throwing punches at each other across the bar.

"Get the peelers, get the peelers." shouted the barman. Collins landed a punch on his head and Jackson caught him back in return, but Collins did what he did to a lot of men in bars and elsewhere, knocked him cold.

Well, a policeman was always expected to handle himself, on or off duty, day or night. Jackson lay in a heap crumpled on the floor. "I think I will get that train now and if he gives any more trouble when he wakes up, get the police straight away." Collins puts on his jacket and leaves the pub quietly with no fuss. Standing at the top of the town next to the courthouse he was looking down at the town, his face swollen and slightly bruised after this fighting encounter with Alexander Jackson, thankfully for him it was Jackson who came out worse. Collins surveyed the neat and tidy little streets of this pretty market town, he turned and started walking along John Street and then James Street where he could see the grey granite building of the railway station. On reaching the front of the road the thin man who sat watching him in the public house tapped Collins on the shoulder. As he spoke he eyed the crowds nervously.

"Sgt. Collins, I might be able to help you with information." Collins turned and stared back at the man.

"I don't think so, I'm about to catch the train back to Sixmilecross, if you have any information then call into Omagh barracks." He was just about to go to the platform to get the train when the man blurted out;

"I can tell you where to find Frankie McPhilips."

Collins spun round. "Who are you? and how do you know about him? Who sent you?"

"My name is John Quinn, that's all you need to know; now calm down and I will tell you what I know." The Sixmilecross train stood hissing in the station, ready to depart.

"Oh bugger, I will get the next one," he mumbled. Then he grabbed John by the lapels and marched him back to a shop doorway on James Street. "Now tell me what you know."

"I can't say too much in the street, we need to go where nobody can hear what I have to say, how much can you pay me?" Collins was irked.

"I should have known it was money you were after; how do I know you're telling the truth?"

"Trust me, it will be worth it, look I only need a few shillings for a few pints of porter or stout." Collins calmed down.

"Alright we will go to the barracks here in the town and you can tell me what you know."

CHAPTER FIFTEEN

John Quinn sat in a small cramped chair in the back room of the barracks, smoking and feeling nervous. Collins sat directly in front of him, nobody else was present, it was a conversation between both men and both men alone. "This is just between the two of us; our chat won't go any further. All I want to do is find Frankie or what's left of him." John listened and spoke.

"I don't know who the people are who took him; I only know it was something to do with dispute over money, but I discovered what had happened in a bar in Beragh. I like a drink and I will go to any pub for a tipple," he continued. "I was lying with my head on the bar sleeping after drinking one stout too many when two men sat talking next to me, both of them were seriously drunk and this loosened their conversation a bit too much, so I pretended that I was still asleep and lay listening in to them, they said Frankie owed them money £30.

"I think he told them to leave him alone, so they decided to take him and beat him up and get the money that way. They pretended to be police but when he refused to pay, the men took him to Pigeon Top outside Omagh and shot him, he is buried in a bog hole on Pigeon Top and I have been up there, and I think I know where he is. That's all I can tell you." Collins was pleased.

"That's all I need to know, if I can find his body and bring it back home to his family for a proper Christian burial, then I will have done my work." Both men got up. "We need to go there to Pigeon Top before it gets dark and see if we can find his body." As they got to the door of the barracks, Inspector O'Callahan calls in to collect some files. He meets Collins and Quinn as he walks in. "Inspector O'Callahan can you help me? I need you to join us and find an ordinary motor car, not a Crossley as we don't want to draw any attention to us and I need two constables who are not in uniform to come along also." O'Callahan looked perturbed.

"Why, what is wrong?" he inquired.

"I can't say too much Sir, but remember that morning last November, when a farmer, Frankie McPhilips, went missing?" He paused for breath. "Well I think I know where he is." O'Callahan jumped into action.

"You two get some civvy clothes on and come with us, we need some sack cloth, rope, some shovels, and a grappling hook. There is a photo of Frankie McPhilips in the public office, we will bring that too so we can identify him, and we'll borrow the District Inspector's motor car."

Pigeon Top is a stretch of moor and bog land about four miles from Omagh, at the top of the hill stands Pigeon Top forest. The commandeered District Inspector's motor car was soon reaching the Straduff Road near the area where John Quinn suggested they would find Frankie's body. They stopped the car at the edge of the road. "The bog hole is over there. I know this place like the back of my hand, I used to come up here as a child and I worked up here as a forester before I started drinking stout too much."

He stretched his right arm in the direction that the men should walk. "Follow me," and he set off across the marshy ground, with the four plain-clothed policemen walking behind him, and gripping on to their equipment for the grisly task. The men were soon caked in soft marshy mud, it covered their clothes in the wet sticky substance, and they threw the grappling iron down to the bottom of the hole and dragged it from one part of the earth to the other side of this watery pit.

"We have hooked something on the bottom," said O'Callahan.

"Yes I feel it, we have caught something," said one of the constables. Slowly an arm began to emerge from the watery tomb. Collins waded in and stood behind the body, he reached for the head and pulled at the chin with both hands, bringing the corpse towards the edge of the bank and solid ground. The corpse lay fully clothed and lifeless on the grass as a lamp was shone on the face, it matched the photo – it was indeed Frankie's body. The peaty water of the bog had preserved him well, and the bullet wounds were present, one on the forehead and four in the chest area. The corpse was then wrapped in the rough brown sack that they brought from the barracks.

"We will take his body to the mortuary at the county infirmary." O'Callahan took out a big pound note and handed it to John Quinn. "Thank you for your help in finding Frankie's body, it's just a pity that his mother isn't around to bring him home, she died a few months ago but at least now they will be buried together." They put the sack-wrapped corpse onto the back seat of the car and took it back to Omagh and on to the hospital. "You can get out of the car, John, before we get to the town." The car lurched to a stop and John Quinn got out without saying a word.

"I'd put any money on that he's going to the nearest public house," said Collins.

"Poor bastard, what a way to live," said O'Callahan. "All he's doing is topping up the alcohol, he'll be dead in no time living like that. Oh, Sergeant, don't worry about getting the next train, we will leave you back to Sixmilecross." said O'Callahan.

Frankie was left lying on the slab in the ice-cold morgue, the doctor would check his wounds and try and confirm the cause of death the next morning.

The car was making its way to the village in the darkness of the late evening but before they could reach the relative safety a road block came into view, the four policemen in the car reached in panic for their hidden pistols and gripped them tightly with nervous anticipation, the men on the roadblock did the same. The briefest moment of shock on both sides turned into screaming and utter pandemonium as both groups of men began shouting for the other.

"Stop, you bastards or we will shoot," shouted both parties. The men on the roadblock jerked their weapons up into firing positions, and fingers grew taut on the triggers, the men on the roadblock pointed their rifles and roared again, "Get out of the fucking car!"

The standoff lasted only twenty seconds, but it seemed like a very long time. Time in fact seemed to slow down. Collins decided to take a chance in the darkness, it was hard to know who was stopping them, and so his next words could mean either bullet in the brain for all of them, or safety.

"Don't shoot, we're the RIC, police on duty."

Then a strong Belfast voice answered; "Special Constabulary on duty."

"Thank fuck for that," said Collins, in a relieved voice. O'Callahan wasn't pleased with the behaviour of the Special Constables, but he bit his lip and kept his emotions to himself.

"Where are you going to?" asked a Special, as more of the heavily armed Special Constables surrounded the car.

"We are going to Sixmilecross Barracks," said Collins.

"You better be careful, lads, it's been attacked again by the IRA tonight."

Collins looked worried. "Anybody hurt?" he asked.

"Two constables killed," he answered. Collins sank in down in his seat. Not again, he thought.

"All right, boys, let them pass," said the Special.

The large patrol of Specials stood and watched the car pass by with a certain amount of contempt.

"What do you think, boys?" said one.

"Bunch of Sinn Feiners," said the other Special. They all roared and laughed at that remark, as they watched the car continue onto the village.

"Did you notice anything about those Special

Constables, Collins?" said O'Callahan, as they drove slowly down the road past them.

"No Inspector, what did you notice?"

"They are not the Tyrone men that we are used to, they are all coming down from Belfast. I'm telling you, something big is going on with this partition talk, Collins, and we are the meat in the sandwich."

As the car arrived back in the village the damage to the barracks was quite extensive. Collins walked in through the broken main door, and a shocked-looking Whelan was standing at the shattered desk in the public office.

"What happened?" he asked.

Whelan composed himself, "A large force of IRA attacked us, they used a potato sprayer with petrol to douse the front door, and then they set it alight."

"The two new constables, O'Dywer and Mc Connell, tried to put out the fire and both were shot dead. The rest of us got out the back and hid in the parade ground, the IRA men got in and stole all the rifles, before the Specials came in and chased them away, plus two more constables have resigned so we are down to the bare bones, sir." Collins felt demoralized but he didn't show it.

"Constable Whelan let's get this place cleaned up, get what is left of the men to assemble in the public office now, I need to speak to them." He turned and went outside to inform the inspector waiting in the car of this worsening situation. "Sir, we need more rifles, the IRA took the lot in the raid, and can you get me four or five constables from Omagh? It will only be temporary until replacements come."

"Alright Sergeant let me get back to Omagh, and I will have more sent over within the hour, but it will be hard, as I'm starting to run out of temporaries and replacements. Right, Constable, let's go," he said, and the motor car rattled away back down the Omagh Road.

"Sergeant Collins, a circular arrived for you this afternoon from RIC HQ in Dublin. I managed to save it before the attack started," said Whelan. Collins opened the letter, he studied it in disbelief and shook his head.

"HQ has just informed me and every other policeman in Ireland that from today the RIC are no longer to wear numerals on their tunics, so take them off now." The men removed them straight away with no fuss. "You know what this means to us in Ulster? The Special Constabulary don't wear numerals, so as from today we will be indistinguishable from them." Collins put the letter in his pocket. "Men that will be all, carry on with the clean-up, I shall be in my office if you need me," and he walked sullenly away to send his reports to RIC HQ and Dublin Castle.

CHAPTER SIXTEEN

SIXMILECROSS, IRELAND

JULY 1921

The men in the barracks were woken late at night to a loud desperate knocking at the front door. "Help us, please help us," they cried. Whelan dashed to the door and peered slowly out the window – it could be a trap. However, it was the owner and barman of Blaney's, a public house at the bottom of the street.

"You better come in," said Whelan. Collins met them as he came down the stairs, quickly buttoning up his tunic.

"What is the problem, men?" he asked.

"I was standing looking out the window of the pub when I saw a carload of Specials pulled up outside. I noticed they had only their sidelights of the motor car on then two of them got out and started banging on the window, shouting 'Open up, police open up now.'" Both men had strong Belfast accents. "They began to hammer the door so in a panic we got out the back window and came up to you in the barracks." Collins grabbed his rifle.

"Whelan go up to the sleeping quarters and wake the day shift men up, tell them to get dressed and get the rest of the boys ready." Collins picked up the telephone to ring Inspector O' Callaghan in Omagh Barracks. The Inspector came to the phone. "Sorry to ring you at this time, Inspector, but I am having more bother with the Special Constabulary again, they are searching a store in the village for guns. Can you come straight away? I am getting my men ready to go up and see what is happening."

"Yes," said O' Callaghan, "I am on my way." The RIC immediately to investigate Collins grabs his men and propels them out the door and down the dark street towards the spirit grocers store. As the RIC men approach the pub they can see the dark shapes of the Specials. Collins shouts a warning, "Police on duty, stop what you are doing." The Specials are conducting searches for weapons, the public house is believed to be a haunt for active Republicans in this part of Tyrone. The Specials Sergeant calls back to Collins;

"We have expressed authority to conduct our own searches as a police force without having to notify you in the barracks. We have found guns on the property of the public house, the two men you have back at the barracks need to be arrested now." Collins barked back;

"Do not tell me who can or cannot be arrested, I will decide." The situation is tense and suddenly a shot was fired from somewhere. The two startled opposing police forces drop to the ground as bullets pop around them.

Bullets pop and ping all around them. "Fuck me what are they doing?" said Collins as a storm of bullets rain more lead on the RIC men cowering on the ground. Collins fires off a few rounds, hitting a Special in the shoulder, spraying the nearest wall in terrible pink, the Special stumbles forward and crumples under the Sergeant's well-aimed shot as the sour fumes of cordite and gunfire drift in the air. The men with rifles in hand scramble around, looking for a better position to return fire, sending firestorms of hot intense volleys of lead back and forward at each other, the fire fight is fierce and short. Collins lies on his back and tries to take control of the situation.

"EVERYBODY STOP SHOOTING!" he roars. "Stop shooting, ceasefire, CEASEFIRE!" His men comply and hold their fire and gradually and slowly the gunfire stops, the shooting was over. One Special is wounded in the shoulder and none of the RIC patrol is injured. When the police enter the pub, they find three more Specials, one of them is standing by the door shaking his head. Collins approaches him.

"What the fuck was that about, Constable?" The constable answers in a slight voice.

"We were informed that there were guns hidden on the premises, we have done nothing wrong, Sergeant."

"It's not right for policemen to shoot at each other – we are all on the same side." Inspector O' Callaghan arrives in the police motor car from Omagh – he is not happy, not happy at all. Lord Copeland has also arrived, he walks slowly to O' Callaghan.

"Your men were conducting a police operation without my knowledge," said O' Callaghan.

Copeland stayed calm. "You might be the Police Inspector for this part of Tyrone but you are now speaking to the Member Of Parliament for this area and I demand you show me more respect." O' Callaghan fumed at that cutting remark.

"Alright then Mr Important, what are you going to do about your men?" Lord Copeland paused in thought.

"I will do nothing. My Specials raided a public house belonging to a Republican Publican." Copeland smiled. "Try saying those two words together with a few drinks taken." The Specials all laughed at his little joke. Lord Copeland pointed to his men. "Go back to my estate, immediately, and fetch the doctor for my wounded constable. I will speak to you all when I get home." They drive out of the village, back to the estate.

"I am not letting this go," said O' Callaghan. Lord Copeland takes out a cigarette and lights it.

"Inspector O' Callaghan I would advise you not to take this incident any further, it was a mistake, a blue-on-blue accident between two patrols who both made an error of judgement." Lord Copeland gets back into the car and his driver throttles past O' Callaghan and Collins.

"That told him," said Collins.

"I don't think so, Sergeant." said O' Callaghan "We are losing our authority with every day that passes, Copeland is a dangerous man – a very dangerous man." All the men make their way back to the barracks and they are no sooner inside when they receive important news from Dublin. Collins read it as follows:

"The news from Dublin Castle today, a truce between Dail Eireann and the British Government has been agreed by both sides in the conflict to facilitate peace talks between the two warring parties, the truce will come into effect at midnight tonight."

"A truce – it won't be worth the paper it is written on in Ulster, you just wait and see," said O'Callahan glumly.

*

A few days later Collins decides to find out if his transfer to Cork was back on again as he felt the truce might have created a chance of him getting moved nearer to home. The truce was being observed in the southern counties of Ireland but for Tyrone and the northern counties, there was no such peace and the fighting continued as usual. He hadn't had any news in months, so on his day off he calls in to Omagh Barracks to find out. O'Callahan meets him in the public office, he was looking worse than the last time Collins had seen him.

"Hello Inspector, I have called in to find out, have you heard anything about my transfer to Cork?" O'Callahan shook his head.

"There is no word of your move, Sergeant, but somebody is getting a transfer that they didn't look for and they will be moving next week."

"I don't understand, sir, who is getting transferred?"

"It's me; I'm getting moved next week to Tramore, County Waterford."

Collins stood open mouthed and speechless, it takes him a few minutes to respond. "Tramore in Waterford, that's hundreds of miles away, it's seven hours on the train, something is up, this is crazy, I mean, you might as well be on the moon." The Inspector agreed.

"I have been banished as far away from Ulster as possible, and I know why and by whom."

"Why do you think it has happened, sir?" asks

Collins.

"It is very simple: I reported the Special Constabulary for their behaviour that night and for other serious incidents, to RIC headquarters and Dublin Castle, Lord Copeland warned me not to do so, he knew I didn't listen to him, so he got his own back."

"The slimy bastard, imagine stitching you up like that for just doing the right thing," said Collins.

"Politicians don't have any morals, Sergeant, you should know that by now. They will do anything to stay in power and in charge and they will do or say one thing and mean another. Remember in history, Julius César, the same people become politicians now as in the ancient days of Greece and Rome. I told you he was a dangerous man and I have been proven right again, please be wary when I'm in Waterford, Sergeant Collins. Be very careful of him as I fear you could be next on his list."

CHAPTER SEVENTEEN

SIXMILECROSS, IRELAND

AUGUST 1921

Under a warm sweltering afternoon sun, Collins and his six-man patrol walked the beat of the main street. He walked a bit behind his constables, chatting to the shopkeepers that had come out to see the local policemen on duty.

"What's this all about?" said Whelan jokingly. "There are far too many of us on the beat, it looks stupid."

"Orders are orders," joked O' Malley.

"These uniforms are useless, it's too hot to wear tunics today," said Whelan. The men continued their beat as the sun blazed down. Collins stopped at another shop.

"What a beautiful day, sir," he said to the owner. "Ah yes, it is, Sergeant, we must make the most of it as in Ireland the rain is never far away," he joked.

Two miles east of Sixmilecross, three men were

loosening the tracks of the railway line at the part where the line ran along a raised embankment, two more men who were acting as scouts on the nearby hillside kept a look out for police, military, and specials. "We will show them what we think of the truce," one laughed, as they used iron bars to tear the tracks out of the ground. Once the loosened length of rail was removed, the men placed two land mines on the track.

"Let's get back up to the safety of the top of the hill, derailing a train at this spot would cause the most damage as the train will roll down the steep embankment," said the IRA man as they all made their way to wait for the train. The train was soon speeding and puffing down the rail line to Sixmilecross station, it was only minutes away. "Steady boys, wait until the engine and some of the carriages pass over the mines then we will explode them." It was now 3.34 p.m., the engine and the first four carriages managed to jump the missing rail, but the fifth carriage ploughed into the ground and caught the full blast of the mines, setting off a huge explosion that shattered the wooden carriages, showering wood, fuel, fire, and human and animal body parts all over the embankment. Curses, men's screams, and the horrific sound of horses in panic and distress filled the air, the train made a grinding metallic sound as it twisted and rolled down the bank. Steam hissed and belched, sounding like the death throes of a great dragon. The noise of the explosion carried into the village and everybody on the street turned in horror in the direction of the terrible cacophony.

"Oh bollox that was a fucking huge bang, it must be a bomb," said Whelan.

"Quickly men, get in to the Crossley and let's find out where that explosion has come from," said Collins. The men all jump into the car and take off as fast as the vehicle can travel, towards the area of the attack. Horses and men lie dead, some bodies were charred and torn like shreds of paper and the contents of the train were tossed and ripped apart, lying strewn on the ground. The rest of the cavalry troop wanders around, bloodied and dazed. At the bottom of the embankment twenty wagons containing horses and men of the 15th Hussars, who were travelling from Belfast to Galway and passing through Tyrone, came to rest in a mangled heap of destruction due to the violence of a human-made storm. The explosion caused the wagons with the cavalry on board to telescope and derail down the embankment. Collins reached the bottom of the steep bank where the train had come to rest as he gazes in disbelief at the carnage right in front of him.

"How many dead?" he asked a trooper.

"We think eight of our men are dead, but there could be more." The sound of horses in distress filled the air. Whelan runs towards the wagons where the terrible sounds are emanating from and climbs on top of the damaged carriages.

Troopers and the policemen cover their ears, the sounds of badly injured horses were too awful to listen to.

"Sgt. we need to do something to put them out of their misery," Whelan walked over with tears in his eyes. "They are too badly injured to be saved, we are going have to shoot them." The troopers broke down and cried but they knew it had to be done.

"I had that horse with me in the great war," said one. The men were reluctant to shoot but their bullets ripped into the animal's flesh and silenced the terrible whines forever as one by one they put them out of their misery. Lord Basil Copeland and his Special Constables soon arrived at the scene. He didn't speak but his face hardened as he surveyed the shocking scene of carnage, dead troopers, and horses of his old regiment lay scattered over the grass. As he stood next to Collins he looked him up and down with distain then he called his specials over towards him.

"That's it now, boys, we have been on the defensive for so long now, so we are not putting up with this bullshit any longer! We are going on the offensive, hit back and hit hard, it's an eye for an eye from this moment on!" Captain Rupert Cavandish

Jones was also in a rage as he marched a party of civilians from the nearby countryside, they were there to dig a large burial pit to put the horses in. "Alright you Irish layabouts, take your spades and start digging, we must bury these poor animals slaughtered by these fiends and rotters." Collins walks over to Lord Copeland.

"Why did you get Inspector Jerimiah O'Callahan transferred to the other end of the country in Waterford?"

"I don't know what you are talking about, Sergeant."

"Yes you do!" Collins says angrily.

Copeland hit back, "Now listen to me, Collins, that man O'Callahan was a trouble-maker from the start, he had it coming and, another thing, what do you mean the other end of the country? The south of Ireland will soon be a different country, we are creating our own nation, staying within the British Empire up here in Ulster, and it will be called Northern Ireland. Personally I can't stand the name myself, using the name Ireland makes us sound like we want to be Irish which I can tell you, we are certainly not! I wanted to call the new country North East Ulster but I got voted down by my fellow MPs in the new Northern Parliament in Belfast City Hall, and the last thing I will say to you is the same thing that I told O'Callahan – just you be careful and watch what you say and do around here, there is a new show in charge and it won't be Dublin Castle running it for much longer!" Copeland walked away from Collins in a bad temper, he goes over to speak with Captain Rupert who is standing with one foot perched on one of the dead horses' backs, smoking a cigarette.

"Right boys, there is the cottage, let's go and see who is at home." The Black and Tans had reached the home of a local rebel supporter, a quaint one-story whitewashed stone-walled cottage with a sandy-yellow thatched roof and a bright red door. "Put your boot through the door." yelled a tan, and the wooden door was smashed to the ground, splintering into hundreds of pieces. As it crashed down the men poured in through the opening, smashing crockery off the walls. "Search every part of the house, if we find anyone just shoot them, boys," said another angry tan.

They threw the kitchen table against the wall and broke all the chairs. Using their rifle butts they nosily broke all the glass from the windows.

"No sign of anybody, sir."

"It's lucky for them that there is nobody home!" The Black and Tans commander ordered his men outside, they went to the Crossley and took out a can of petrol.

"Now men, let's burn it down." Petrol is poured on the thatched roof and all over the broken furniture and a burning torch is thrown into the property, with a loud whoosh and a roar, the cottage takes light and goes up in flames. Some of the Black and Tans were not happy about having to wreck homes in such a terrible fashion, but all reprisals were sanctioned by the British Government in Westminster. The Black and Tans always carried out their wartime orders.

They all stand and watch it burn, one of the tans laughs. "I feel a song coming on, boys, and we all know the words, it goes like this: *"Keep the home fires burning while our hearts are yearning, tho you may be far away, I think of you."* They all hum the tune as they get into the Crossley and drive back to their headquarters, pleased with the work they have done, behind them the red glow of the fire and the dark black smoke can be seen for miles around. This was a reprisal for the troop train attack and it wouldn't be the last.

CHAPTER EIGHTEEN

SIXMILECROSS, IRELAND

OCTOBER 1921

A gunmetal grey sky threatened more rain, but Collins wasn't bothered as he stood out at the front door of the barracks and watched the convoy of trucks and Crossleys driving more reinforcements of Special Constabulary through the village. Whelan came out and joined his sergeant viewing the spectacle.

"Where are they going sir?" he asked.

"Those men have been training in Newtownards and Belfast for a number of weeks now, Whelan. They have decided to create a border between the six northern counties and the twenty-six southern counties." Whelan looked confused.

"I thought Ulster had nine counties?"

"Yes, it does, but the unionists have worked out that nine counties is too much ground to hold on to and too many nationalists to contain, so they can have a better and bigger majority of unionists in six of the counties. Those Special Constables are driving to the edge of what they call the six plantation counties, which are Derry, Tyrone, Fermanagh, Down, Armagh, and Antrim to reinforce the border."

"It's amazing," said Whelan. "We have only six RIC men in this barracks but the Special Constabulary get bigger and bigger." Collins watched the convoy drive out of the village.

"They are driving to Strabane and Enniskillen, the nearest towns of this newly created border, at the moment the border is just in the minds of the unionist politicians like Lord Basil Copeland and I hope that is where it stays!" The convoy rumbled on and both men walked back indoors to the warm turf fire of the public office out of the cold chill of the October afternoon. The rest of the men sat at the table smoking cigarettes and playing cards, the telephone rings and Whelan answers it.

"I have had a report of men seen with rifles at the top of the hills overlooking the Tiroony Road, Sergeant, what shall I tell the caller?" he asked. Collins takes the phone off him.

"Men with rifles, we don't have enough constables here to deal with the incident, I will give you the number of Lord Basil Copeland's private home and he will get a party of Black and Tans to deal with it instead," and he put the phone down. Collins was raging as he should be dealing with this report now, but his hands are tied. "I feel so useless, boys, we are policemen who have pledged to uphold and defend the law and we can't do a bloody thing."

"It's awful," said O' Malley, as he threw down his set of cards on the table.

"What a useless hand that was," he complained.

"I couldn't win an argument." The men all laugh and Collins heads upstairs to have a lie down. He feels his power as a policeman is ebbing away.

"If anything happens, boys, will you call me?"

"Yes Sarge, no problem," they said. Whelan shuffles the deck.

"All I can say is, we are indoors in a nice warm room playing cards, drinking tea, and most importantly we are not out getting are heads shot off."

"I agree," says O' Malley. He looks at his deck of cards and smiles into himself and thinks, *That's a good hand, my luck has changed in this game.* Collins lies on the top of his bed thinking about his situation, all this talk of partition and two parliaments in Ireland spins around in his head.

"The chances of me getting back to Cork in this job were very slim if not impossible, and it's going to be impossible to go home now, as if I resign from the RIC, I will be classed as a traitor and shot, I just don't know what to do anymore. I'm dammed if I leave the job and dammed if I don't." He felt like a bird trapped in a cage.

*

The four Crossleys were full of Black and Tans and Auxiliaries from Donegal. They were on their way to the homes of known Sinn Fein supporters; the cottages were spread out over a six-mile radius just outside of the village of Beragh. "We will soon be at the houses," said one. The men felt safe enough to travel by road in broad daylight. It would have been too dangerous to travel the same way only a few months ago, day or night, but the IRA was now on the back foot. The truce was only relevant in the southern counties of Ireland and in Ulster the fighting continues, just the same as before the 11th of July truce.

"Right men, search the houses and if you find anyone make them stand outside." The Black and Tans go through the homes, smashing pictures of Michael Collins and Éamon De Valera, along with which holy statues come crashing down as they march everyone out of their houses.

"You had something to do with the train attack," one Tan says in an angry Essex accent to four men found cowering in the kitchen.

"Put them up against the stone wall and search them, I'd bet those were the bastards that blew up the troop train a few months ago," said another Special.

A can of Petrol is poured into the cottage, the red and orange flames burst out, engulfing the building and roof like a bonfire as the evening sky is lit up in a bright crimson glow. The men all stand with fear in their eyes and their hands up, reaching for the sky. The Black and Tans open fire, raking them with bullets and they drop beneath the wall screaming, bleeding, and dying, snarling like mad dogs with teeth barred and writhing in agony. Then suddenly the screams stop and the only sound to be heard is the noise of the cottage burning.

CHAPTER NINETEEN

Darkness hid a convoy of Auxiliary vehicles as they rumbled along the road, the men sat with determined faces ready to wreak their revenge on the nationalist population again. A special constable and an RIC constable were shot dead by the IRA the previous night and now the nationalists of Beragh village were going to pay for it. The Crossleys arrived into town and the silence of the dark night was broken by the sounds of hobnail boots on the cobble streets.

"Go and check the pub and the grocery shop next door for Sinn Feiners," said an Auxiliary. Nobody was there, so both buildings were set alight. Both shops crackled and burned fiercely as the flames shot into the air. They moved to the next property and stood pouring volley after volley of shots through the windows of the house. An Auxiliary stood firing his heavy Lewis machine gun into the property and metallic splinters ripped through the walls and windows in a hellish hailstorm of metal. "I don't care who is in the house, it must be done," he said, "as these people are in the IRA, this is a one hundred per cent Sinn Fein house!"

House after house was ransacked and the furniture thrown into the street and set on fire. Once the town was on fire, the Auxiliaries turned their attention to the cottages in the countryside. It was now 3 a.m. as they arrived at the first of them.

"Open the door, police on duty."

A woman's voice answered in return. "Hold on a minute while I find the key," she said.

"We will give you a minute and no more, that is all, so hurry up." Once she got the door opened she stepped back in anticipation of the men coming through the door, but they stepped back into the shadows so she couldn't see them properly.

"Please come in," she suggested.

"No, we won't come in. Send out all the men of the house." The men of the house – John, James, Francis, Matthew, and Michael – stepped outside, eyes wide with fear.

"These men are known to have links with the IRA," said one of the Auxiliaries. "These are definitely the men involved in blowing the train up," he added. "Right boys put your hands up and start walking!" They are marched at gun point down the lane; fear filled the men's bodies as they shake in terror with guns trained on them. About a mile down the road from their house they are ordered to stop. "Stop here, next to the grass bank." The men do what they are told, and then suddenly rifle and pistol fire hammers down on them, tearing holes in their bodies, each one springing what seemed like hundreds of leaks as blood sprays everywhere. The men don't get a chance to cry out or speak, but now they lie quiet and still in a crumpled heap, dead, after being lined up against a bank on a dark lonely hollow in the road and riddled with bullets.

Bullets have shattered the men's heads, chests, and they all have large gaping stomach wounds. There were no survivors in the murderous attack. The cottage isn't burned this time, shooting the men of the house was punishment enough but the fiery glow of Beragh lit up the night sky for miles around.

"It is the only way to show that these rebels won't be tolerated in Ulster, no surrender and no Sinn Fein in Ulster," was the cry from the Auxiliaries as they left the scene of destruction.

*

The following morning arrived bright and clear. Sgt. Collins stood behind the desk in the public office, he was in deep conversation with Constable Whelan.

"We are waiting for the new replacements to arrive

from the train, we have four new constables arriving from the training depot HQ at Phoenix Park in Dublin, that means we now have only six policemen instead of eight to cover the barracks and surrounding areas." The four smartly dressed men march into the front office with their suitcases. Collins stretches out his hand to welcome them.

"My name is Constable Peter Mc Donagh from Mayo." The rest of the men give their names also.

"Constable Patrick Kenny from Dublin."

"Constable Michael Cleary from Louth."

"Constable Sean O' Connor from Sligo."

"Welcome to Sixmilecross, men. Constable Whelan will show you to your sleeping quarters." Before Whelan could do this a man comes running into the office.

"Sgt. Collins we have a fight on the main street, come quick." Collins comes out from behind the desk.

"Have you any idea who is fighting?" he asked.

"I don't know one of the men, but the other man is Alec Jackson." Collins shook his head.

"Well fuck me, Alexander Jackson again, what a surprise. I've got you now this time, Alec. Whelan, come with me," he orders, and both men run out through the door. Collins turns to speak to his newly arrived constables, he points his finger at them and shakes it.

"Men stay there, we will show you to your quarters when we get back." They bolt down the street towards the excitement. Alexander Jackson stands over the man he has just beaten up a few minutes ago. He is a tough fighter and it was no shame for any man to go down at his hands, he turns around to see Collins and Whelan blocking his escape. There isn't the usual smile from Jackson for Collins this time, but he is still smartly dressed like a Chicago gangster.

"Sgt. Collins, I have a very bad memory of the last time we met in a pub in Omagh." he growled. Collins smirked. He remembered it well also.

"You didn't remember too much after I caught you with my right hook." Jackson walks up to Collins and goes nose to nose with him.

"Don't worry there will be a price to pay for what happened you'll see."

"Don't try and intimidate me, you jumped up prick," said Collins as he grabs him by the jacket and Whelan catches him by the neck. All three men then crash down onto the street.

"Calm down, fer fuck sake, calm down," says Whelan, as they writhe and wrestle for control. "Get the handcuffs on him. Get the handcuffs on him!" Jackson puts up the fight of his life on the Sixmilecross street, then the newly arrived constables come outside to see what is happening and they come down and overpower Jackson.

"What are you arresting me for?" he questions as he is bundled by the uniformed and non-uniformed officers.

"Alec where do I start?" said Collins. "This time I'm going to throw the book at you," he says. "You assault a man on the street, you resisted arrest, you assault six policemen, myself included." Collins kicks the front door of the barracks, damaging the panel. "There is another charge, Alec, damaging police property." He is carried in and hauled into the cell and the big heavy door is slammed shut behind him. "Now you will stay there while I prepare the charges against you," Collins barked. "Whelan, contact the County Inspector. We are going to ask for a special sitting in Omagh court this evening. I will be in my office to get the paperwork ready. We have got him now for sure." All the policemen were delighted. "That's that bastard going away for a long time; he will be in the jailhouse now, thank God."

*

Collins was happy; he finally had his old enemy bang to rights now. Collins walked out of Omagh Court House later that evening a pleased man. Career criminal Alexander Jackson was sent to Crumlin Road jail in Belfast for six months.

"That's a big load off my mind and one more dangerous man off the streets," he says to Constable O' Connor, whose first job was to accompany Collins to the court session. The new County Inspector meets them at the door of the court.

"A job well done, Sgt. Collins," he says. "I'm Inspector Wilson from Antrim." Collins shakes his hand.

"It's nice to meet you, sir."

"Sgt. Collins a letter has arrived for you at Omagh Barracks from HQ in Dublin – it's very official looking," he said. Collins takes the letter.

"Thank you, sir, I will read it when I get back to Sixmilecross." Collins and O' Connor both get into their car and drive back to the village. As soon as they return, Collins heads straight to his office alone. He doesn't speak as he rushes in to find his paper opener, the letter states:

FROM ROYAL IRISH CONSTABULARY HEADQUATERS DUBLIN CASTLE 20TH NOVEMBER 1921 TO SERGEANT PATRICK JOSEPH COLLINS, WE ARE PLEASED TO INFORM YOU THAT YOU HAVE BEEN PROMOTED TO HEAD CONSTABLE AND HAVE BEEN ACCEPTED FOR TRANSFER FROM SIXMILECROSS RIC BARRACKS COUNTY TYRONE TO BALLINHASSIG RIC

BARRACKS COUNTY CORK. YOUR NEW POST BEGINS ON THE 1ST OF FEBUARY 1922. CONGRATULATIONS ON YOUR TRANSFER AND PROMOTION FROM ALL YOUR COMRADES AT RIC HQ DUBLIN.

He stares down again at the words of the letter; he has finally got the move he has worked for.

"Constable Whelan can you come here please?" he shouts. Whelan runs into the sergeant's office.

"Is something wrong, sir?" Collins stands with the official letter in his hand, smiling with a broad grin.

"Keep it to yourself, Whelan, I have got the promotion and transfer I requested and have been waiting for, this past year or so." Whelan extends his hand out, offering congratulations.

"Well done, Sergeant, well done," he exclaimed. Collins smiles, he is finally going home to Cork.

"I'm going to pack my case," he said excitedly.

"Fer fuck sake, you're not going for three months," said Whelan, looking at the letter.

"I know that, but I will leave it at the foot of my bed just to remind me that it is really happening. I'm going home to Cork for sure!"

CHAPTER TWENTY

SIXMILECROSS, NORTHERN IRELAND

6TH DECEMBER 1921

Morning arrived; cold, clear, and bright, the sun was shining, and frost clung to the grass. Sergeant Collins had called his men to a meeting in the public office of the barracks, the front door was locked shut, it would only open in an emergency. The mood of the men was sombre and Collins stood with an official document in his hand, he had an hour to study the contents of the document and it made for grim reading. Collins was shaken up by what it said. "Men, I have news on the peace talks that were taking place in Downing Street between the imperial government and the Irish delegation, a peace treaty was signed early this morning by Michael Collins and Prime Minister Lloyd George, they have agreed to the partition of Ireland, creating two parliaments, one in Dublin and one in Belfast."

Sgt. Collins drew breath. "The Parliament in Belfast will govern six of Ireland's counties: Fermanagh, Tyrone, Antrim, Down, Derry, and Armagh and will be called Northern Ireland. It will remain part of the United Kingdom and the British Empire. The southern parliament will govern twenty-six of Ireland's counties from Dublin, it will be called the Irish Free State and will have dominion status like Canada or New Zealand and its members of parliament, or TDs as they like to be called, will have to swear an oath to the King." Whelan raised his hand.

"What does that mean for us sir?" Collins looked up from the document.

"I'm coming to that now, Whelan," he said. "Both Unionist and Nationalist governments in Belfast and Dublin have agreed to the disbandment of the Royal Irish Constabulary as part of the Anglo-Irish treaty and two new police forces are to be set up in Northern Ireland and the Irish Free State."

A huge angry sigh bellowed up from the listening men.

"Disbandment!" said O' Connor.

"Yes boys, I'm sorry but the politicians have decided that we are expendable!" said Collins. "That's it, we can't fight, there is no vote, we are being shut down and done away with." Whelan stood up.

"So that's the thanks we are shown by putting our necks on the line, and risking our lives in the service of the RIC? Good men have died, men that we worked with, and now we find out we meant nothing, it doesn't matter, so what do you think, Sergeant?" Collins rubbed his forehead in worry.

"I agree with you, Constable Whelan, all the politicians, Irish and British, have betrayed us, the bastards have stabbed us in the back, from the minute this trouble started we have been fighting on all fronts. We are Irishmen in the King's Uniform and that made us a target for the rebels who wanted an independent Ireland, and here in Ulster we were hated and mistrusted because we were Catholics. I have done some terrible things, and been to some dark places over the last few years and came back again, I can also say that I'm not the same man I was in 1918 or 1919, our morale has been low up to now, and this news of the disbandment has finished it!" Whelan, Kenny, Cleary, Mc Donagh, and O' Connor all stood up.

Whelan spoke up again, "Sgt. Collins this is the final straw, I'm resigning my post as constable as from now, I will go back to Dublin and get another job if I can, but I don't want to be a policeman anymore. Where does that leave you, Sergeant, what will happen to your transfer and promotion?" Collins looked depressed.

"I have been thinking of my situation since I heard of the signing of the treaty early this morning. I have to be a realist, it won't be happening now, I'm trapped in Tyrone."

"I'm sorry but that's rubbish, sir, you can resign like us," said O' Connor.

"And what do I do, O' Connor? I don't know any job other than a policeman."

"You don't owe anybody anything, Sergeant Collins, just walk away, you have said it yourself, we have all been stabbed in the back!"

"Yes, but despite all that, I have to be true to myself and do my duty." Whelan looked exasperated.

"Ah balls to your duty, we are leaving now, sir, come with us." The men took off their tunics and placed them on the desk in the public office. "We are all resigning our posts as constables with immediate effect!" With all the shouting and heated debate going on in the barracks, nobody heard the sound of a motor car pulling up outside until a heavy knocking sound on the door stopped the men in their tracks. They spun around and reached for their rifles.

"Who is there?" Collins said nervously.

"It's Lord Basil Copeland MP," said the calm voice behind the door.

"The bastard's here to gloat," said Collins quietly to his men. "What do you want, sir?" Collins shouted.

"Open the door now, Green Fella," said Copeland.

"What did he just call me, Whelan?"

"It's your nickname sir, the Green Fella." Collins

opened the door, Lord Copeland stood and grinned, he was smartly dressed in a brown tweed suit and deerstalker hat.

"You know why you are called the Green Fella, Collins? Well, you are related to the gunman who signed the treaty this morning in Downing Street!"

"Nonsense," said Collins. "That's what you tell people, for some reason. Now sir, why are you here?" Copeland produced a large official document from his coat.

"As the member of parliament for this constituency, the government for Northern Ireland here by commandeer all police barracks, for use by the RIC and Ulster Special Constabulary in joint operations, from this date on the seventh of December 1921." Copeland pointed to the waiting carload of Special Constables. "Men, get your equipment ready and make your way inside. Sergeant Collins, you remember some of the boys you met that day? They were sworn in by the Reverend at my estate and I'm placing them under your command until further notice." Collins stood speechless as the Specials jumped up and climbed out of the motor car. "Where are your men going?" Copeland asked.

"They have all resigned, sir, they are leaving on the train when it arrives." Copeland said nothing, but he looked very pleased indeed. The Specials marched into the barracks in their green greatcoats carrying their heavy military holdalls, they swaggered upstairs to the sleeping quarters, past Collins and the departing RIC Constables. Lord Copeland walked into the room

"Sgt. Collins, you have met my men before but permit me to introduce them again, they are Special Constables Laird, Morton, Mills, Lewis, Wilson, and Hall. Hall used to be a sergeant but something happened that I won't discuss with you, he was demoted and here we are. I have put you in charge of the men if you have any problems with them, you just come to me." Collins and Whelan went outside.

"Sgt. resign and come to Dublin with me now on the train, you don't owe these people anything, resign and we will leave, I'm sure my brother will put us up for a few nights," said Whelan. Collins shook his head.

"No I can't go, that means Copeland has won, and I won't let that happen." Whelan gets angry.

"Fer fuck sake, you are one stubborn bastard, Sgt. Collins. Copeland has already won and it's time to get out of here before the worst happens, please, just leave with me now." The Sgt. stepped back onto the steps.

"I'm not going. I can't go and I won't go, for a number of reasons. Firstly, a politician won't put me out. I'm a policeman and I have more morals than

Copeland, I will stay and show him that I'm a better man than him, A BETTER MAN THAN HIM!"

"You know what's going on here, Sgt., did you see the Specials' uniforms? They are green just like the RIC uniform, that's why the numerals were removed from our tunics earlier in the year, they are taking over, and Copeland is running the show." Collins said nothing and Whelan knew that he wasn't going to yield in his stance, so he reached out his hand to him. "Alright Sgt. I'm leaving now, I wish you well, good luck and God bless." Both men shook hands on good terms, Whelan turned in the direction of the train station and Collins went back inside. His eyes were averted to a newly added portrait on the wall.

"What's this?" he asked Laird, who had just come down from the sleeping quarters, pointing at a picture of Edward Carson with the words 'No Home Rule.'

"Oh now, come on Sergeant, you know what they say, Home Rule is Rome Rule," replied Laird.

"So just why exactly do you need pictures like this in a police building?" asked Collins.

"Well Sergeant, it's like this you see, we have created a new country and we can put whatever we like on the wall, in fact, you know, I think we need a portrait of William of Orange crossing the Boyne on his white horse too," said Laird. The other Specials that had just come down the stairs all laughed out loud.

"I also think we will need to fumigate the place, to get rid of all the papist germs," said Hall. The men all laughed again and Collins bit his lip.

"I will be in my office if you are looking for me," and at that Lord Copeland walked out of the barracks, his face flushed with glee.

CHAPTER TWENTY-ONE

ENNISKILLEN, NORTHERN IRELAND

9TH DECEMBER 1921

Collins sat in Blake's of the hollow bar in Enniskillen, he had agreed to catch the train down to the island town to meet ex-constable Liam Whelan. They had chosen Enniskillen, mainly so as Collins could get away from Tyrone for a few hours and escape the prying eyes of the people in Sixmilecross. Whelan walked in to find Collins sitting next to the fire in the big snug, he waved over to Whelan. "Come and join me. Barman, can I have two hot whiskeys please?" Whelan sat down in the small brown seat. "What happened when you got to Dublin?" Collins asked.

"It was a dangerous place for me, it has changed a lot from the last time I went there. I was handed a letter and here it is." He took the letter out of his pocket and handed it to Sergeant Collins, he looked down at the handwritten note and studied the words carefully.

POBLACT NA HEIREANN TO CONSTABLE

LIAM WHELAN RIC, TAKE WARNING, EVEN IF YOU RELINQUISH YOUR PRESENT OCCUPATION OR NOT YOU MUST LEAVE IRELAND WITHIN 72 HOURS OR THE SENTENCE OF DEATH ALREADY PASSED ON YOU WILL BE CARRIED OUT. SIGNED MATT BROGAN COMMANDANT DUBLIN IRA.

Whelan was white with worry but he only wanted to talk about Collins' situation. " You know why Copeland put you in charge of the Specials the other day, it was to undermine your authority, they will pretend that you are in charge but all the time they will answer only to him, you will be a puppet and he will be pulling all the strings. I'm talking to you as a friend now, Pat, you must get out of it, leave and resign now."

"But where will I go?" said Collins. "I can't go to Cork or I will be shot as a traitor, you just missed the bullet yourself in Dublin."

"Yes I know I did, Cork is out of the question also, it is time to move to a new and different country now, so I'm leaving tomorrow and catching the boat to England. I'll find work somewhere, who knows I might even apply for a job as constable again. I hear England is a safe place to work as a policeman, well I mean, it will be easy compared to Ireland that's for sure; you could come with me if you want?"

"And do what?" said Collins indignantly. "No, I'm going to tough it out; I won't be intimidated by them or their ilk." Whelan shook his head back and forward.

"So I can't talk you out of it?"

"No never, if I walk away now Copeland and his men have won." Whelan said nothing, he had tried his best to make Collins change his mind but to no avail, there was nothing he could do, he was staying in Sixmilecross and that was it. Whelan got up from his chair.

"Patrick, I wish you well. I'm leaving shortly for Belfast; I must catch the boat to Liverpool." He held out his hand, but Collins stood up.

"I will walk with you to the train station, I'm going to go back to Omagh and Sixmilecross this evening." Both men walked out the door of William Blake's public house, past the famous red and black front of the building and on to the main street of Enniskillen. The walk took them through the Town Centre, past the shop fronts on High Street, Townhall Street, onto East Bridge Street then Belmore Street and on to the railway station.

*

The six o'clock train to Omagh puffed and chugged as the passengers boarded through the open doors of the carriages. Collins turned to his friend and comrade Liam Whelan, "That's my train now, I must go, Liam."

"Alright Patrick good luck and God bless," he answered.

"And you likewise." Both hugged each other. "This won't be the last time we see each other," said Collins, "write to me at the barracks and send me your new forwarding address and I will come and visit someday." He climbed aboard the train as the guard blew his whistle and closed the door behind him and the train clanked out of Enniskillen. Whelan stood and watched it vanish out of sight.

"Collins is a good friend and I hope he's right about us meeting up again," he said under his breath. The station was extremely busy with all platforms fully utilized so Whelan decided to use the refreshment room with its bar and warm blazing fire.

CHAPTER TWENTY-TWO

A worried-looking Lord Copeland stood in the public office of the barracks, Collins sat on a high chair behind the main desk writing down his complaint. "I want to report the abduction and kidnapping of my dear friend Reverend Samuel Smythe." Collins took a note of the name.

"Lord Copeland, he is not the only one to be kidnapped last night." What had happened was that of a carefully planned operation, the IRA launched simultaneous raids into counties Armagh, Tyrone, and Fermanagh. Their objective was to kidnap several prominent Unionists and hold them hostage. "Does that mean the reverend is a top Unionist?"

"Well of course he is, he works for me and he has just been made the county grand master of the Orange Order in Tyrone and is still a member of the UVF." Collins sat and wrote down more details.

"He is most likely being held against his will

across this new border that was created in Donegal or Sligo, there is honestly not a lot that I can do at the moment, Lord Copeland, I'm just about to send out a patrol." At this, the Special Constables came out of the back room with their rifles clean and gleaming.

"We are going out now, we will be back later!" Lord Copeland and the patrol went outside into the street.

"Don't worry," said Laird, "these abductions sound like desperation, we nearly have the IRA beaten in Northern Ireland and it only takes one more push and they will be finished up here once and for all." The men jumped into the Crossley and went out to patrol, they soon saw Father John Mc Chesney strolling down the main street of the village, he was carrying a black leather bag, the Crossley pulled up alongside of him. "Stop right there!" a voice ordered, and he stood still.

"Gentlemen I must protest, I'm saying a private mass for an old lady who is unwell," he said calmly.

"We don't care, you know what you can do with your mass, or any mass for that matter!" said Hall.

"Check him for weapons," said Laird. Father Mc Chesney stood with his arms up as one of the Specials patted him down. "What is in the bag, priest?" Wilson asked.

"It's just my vestments for saying mass," said Mc Chesney in a slightly agitated voice. Wilson grabbed him by the lapels.

"Now don't make trouble for yourself or you will be sorry!" He was then forced up against the side of the Crossley and slapped around the face. "Search his bag!" The bag was opened and his vestments were thrown on the ground for all to see, every part of the bag was checked but nothing was found. "Right Father you can go on your way." They got back into the motor car and drove out of the village, they had planned to do a patrol and set up a checkpoint on one of the back roads on the outskirts of the village. Father Mc Chesney stuffed the clothing back into the bag and went straight for the front door of the barracks; he walked in to find Sgt. Collins peering out the window.

"You were watching what was happening to me outside, Sgt. Collins?" he said.

"Yes Father. I did see what had happened but there is nothing I can do to stop it, those men are under the control of Lord Copeland and they don't take any notice of what I say, they do their own thing." Collins pointed to the wall. "Take a good look at the wall there, Father, and that will tell you all you need to know about this new country Northern Ireland." The portrait of Edward Carson was still there but now alongside it was an even bigger painting of King William of Orange on his white horse, crossing the Boyne with his sword in hand.

"Father Mc Chesney, I think you would be safer moving to a parish in the new Irish Free State, it's only going to get a lot more dangerous for Catholics living this side of the border."

"And what will you do, Sgt.?" Mc Chesney asked.

"I know it's safer up here than in the Free State as I'd be shot on sight if I went home," he added.

"Yes, that might be true, Collins. I'd sit it out up here until the situation in the Free State improves. I will go on and do my mass. Can you take a note of the incident today and speak to your men?"

"Yes of course, Father, I will speak to them when they get back." Father Mc Chesney stormed out of the building and hurried back to the parochial house, a shaken and worried man. When the Specials marched back in, Collins was waiting for them.

"What do you think you are doing, harassing the parish priest? Father Mc Chesney came in to make a complaint about your conduct towards him."

"We have the power to stop who we want on patrol, and we don't discriminate against anybody, priest or not," said Coulter.

"I notice you have taken his side, Sgt. Collins, well that is no surprise."

"What do you mean by that?" said Collins.

"You know well enough what we mean, you always go to the chapel on a Sunday, you and him are great friends." Collins stood up in anger, ready to answer back but he changed his mind.

"Laird and Coulter take over, I'm going to do a foot patrol on the main street, I will be back in half an hour or so." He puts on his cap in a great hurry and walks outside. He walks down the street in normal police fashion with both hands behind his back, his mind is on Dublin. Today the RIC was being formally disbanded, he had been invited to go but turned down the invitation. Why would I want to go and witness the death of the force?, he thought to himself. With his thoughts drifting all around in his head, it was going to be a lonely foot patrol. I used to like getting out of the way of the men and getting out on the beat, he thought, but now was very different. I have men that I do not have under my command, they won't do a thing I say most of the time, the Royal Irish Constabulary is to disbanded officially today. Now I'm still a proud Irishman, but my country has been partitioned into two states, my surname is Collins and I'm from Cork so everybody thinks I'm related to the big fella Michael Collins … so I don't have a lot to celebrate today.

He walked the full length of the village nodding his head at passers-by as he went along. He still looked smart and proud in his green uniform, his simple whistle in his tunic breast pocket attached to a chain to summon assistance, in his leather pouch the ordinary handcuffs for arresting a violent man, his wooden baton and Webley revolver for extra protection, and if all else failed his two fists to defend himself from any attacker. A policeman should, at all times, be able to handle himself. I can't go back to Cork as my transfer and promotion has been cancelled, so what do I do now?, he thought. One thing I won't do is feel sorry for myself, as that won't get me anywhere, or make one bit of difference to the situation. I have got to be tough, and that's all there is to it!

He reaches the bottom of the road then turns and walks back up the street, towards the barracks. When he reaches the barracks, he flings himself sharply in through the door, startling the Constables who were standing talking among themselves in the main room. "Men, I want you all out on patrol now!" he orders, this time the force of his manner and persuasion was enough for them all to comply. "And I want Special Constable Morton to stay behind and man the desk."

"Yes sir, right now," they all answered, and jumped to attention.

With the men all gone Morton could speak to Collins without getting into trouble with the others.

"Sgt. Collins, what I have to say to you, I will only say once and if you quote me on it, I will deny everything." A surprised-looking Collins sat and listened. "I think you are a fine and decent fellow, even if you are a papist, you are still baptized in Christ and you wear the King's uniform with pride, but you still see yourself as an Irishman and the boys want you out. Ex Sergeant Hall wants your job and I mean, you know yourself that Lord Copeland doesn't like you, so my advice to you is leave and go away to England or America, but for God's sake get away from this place. I mean I think all this trouble has been bullshit myself if I'm honest, but I'm not making up the rules, somebody else is, Sgt. Collins, so for your own sake if nothing else, you should just go." Collins smiled nervously.

"Constable Morton thank you for your concern, but I will tell you the same thing that I have told the other people who have given me advice; I'm not going, I have nowhere to go, I have no choice now, and I'm staying!" Morton sat at the desk and said nothing as Collins got up and walked upstairs, the conversation was over, it will never be mentioned again.

DUBLIN, APRIL 4TH 1922

DISBANDMENT

Sgt. Collins was standing at the back of the parade in the bright but cold April sunshine, watching the proceedings. He was angry and felt sick in the pit of his stomach. The men of the Royal Irish Constabulary were marching around the courtyard of Dublin Castle cheering for the cameras as they passed by the men, who stood cranking metal handles on the side of the heavy brown wooden boxes. Collins turned down his invitation to this sombre event but was ordered to attend by RIC headquarters in the Castle. Watching with a heavy heart he felt like crying but men don't cry, so he just bit his lip and seethed underneath, like a fire trapped behind a large door. *I want to open that door and shoot flames of anger all over the parade square, but I'm better than that, I will just keep my emotions to myself and won't lower myself to show them I'm bothered.* The bright green uniforms paraded in splendid marching formations around the red-brick buildings of Dublin Castle. Khaki-clad British soldiers stood and waved their caps in the air, and cheered the policemen at every opportunity, but in spite of their generous support, Collins couldn't raise a smile or a cheer.

He looked away from the parade and stared at his uniform. I gave my all to this uniform and police force since 1892, he thought, I've seen good times and bad times, but I always thought I'd get through it all, but not this time, this time it really is the end for the RIC. Collins placed his hand on his medals and rubbed them. My medals mean nothing now, he thought, absolutely nothing, just pieces of worthless metal on my chest. The brass band of the RIC stood at the corner of the square playing bright happy tunes to try and make everyone feel better about the situation. *Young May Moon*, the marching song of the RIC, brought smiles and tears to the men at the same time and a Scottish regimental pipe band stirred the blood with tunes of their own, the skirl of Highland Laddie briefly cheered up some of the disbanded policemen but Collins wasn't interested.

Never ever trust a politician, he thought. Every one of them are vermin, they will get you in the end, and they are all the same. I feel betrayed and demoralized by what has happened, the government has stabbed us all in the back, that's the thanks we get for being policemen, maintaining English law in Erin's Isle. The policemen stopped marching and all the music ended. They then took off the green RIC tunics, slowly unbuttoning them for the last time, and then dumping them on the ground in a mass symbolic gesture. Green clothing piled up in folds in the middle of the parade ground. This was too much for Sgt. Collins to stomach and he bowed his head and left quietly, to take off his uniform in a small side room in Dublin Castle. My uniform meant more than for it to lie with the others in heaps on the dusty ground, he thought. Collins folded it up neatly and put it back in his kit bag with great care and reverence, plus nothing has changed in the new country of Northern Ireland, the uniform was the same, unlike the Free State where it was to be the colour blue and called the Civic Guard.

CHAPTER TWENTY-THREE

SIXMILECROSS, NORTHERN IRELAND

3RD MAY 1922

The morning of the 3rd of May began in a blaze of fire in Gortin Glen, creating a grand and awful spectacle, making the heavens a large expanse of lurid flames. The IRA 2nd Northern Division which covered counties Derry and Tyrone were on the offensive. IRA GHQ in Beggars Bush Dublin had authorized to go ahead and attack the forces of the Crown and the Northern State, and the May rebellion had begun. The IRA had five Northern Divisions, and each of their commanders all met together in Clones a month earlier, to plan a military offensive in the six counties in early May. Their aim was twofold: to embarrass, destabilize, and destroy the newly created Belfast government, and aiding the search for IRA unity in the twenty-six counties, in an attempt to stave off civil war between the pro and anti-treaty factions of the organization, making it a truly complicated conundrum.

In their wake, scorched stone farmhouses dotted

the countryside, the executed bodies of the unfortunate occupants lay outside their wrecked dwellings, creating a grotesque aspect to the scenery, and even worse, was the sight from inside the house, of charred bodies and glowing human embers. A Flying Column of at least 200 men marched and slogged along the lane towards Gortin RIC Barracks, they carried unlit torches which were just crude wooden sticks with the top wrapped in sack cloth and soaked in Petrol. Their plan was to burn the building and Gortin Barracks was set to be next on the receiving end of the Column's May Rising. Quietly and with deadly purpose the trench-coated rebels crept into the village, as the unaware policemen rested in blissful ignorance.

"Right boys, light the torches and throw them at the building, we'll soon have the bastards burned out!" The rebels swarmed the village like beetles, hurling their flaming presents at the building.

"Share them among yourselves, ya peelers blagards!" joked one of the attackers, as his lit fuse found a hole in the roof and started a warm fiery glow in the rafters. They then scattered and ran for cover, grabbing their rifles and, without waiting for the stone building to catch fire, the men let lose a thunderstorm of bullets across at the barracks, catching a policeman who was peering out the window and tearing him to ribbons, as his broken damaged body dropped in pieces like rice at a wedding. The constables returned fire on their attackers in a noisy clatter of lead, catching two of them on the head and chest respectively, both men folded down dead like musical accordions. Flames burst out all over the barracks, causing the men inside to run outside, it was most likely better to die in a hail of bullets in the village street, than burn to death in the internal inferno.

The building's remaining seven policemen, four RIC Men and three Special Constables, scrambled and dashed into the street, pulling the wounded with them, returning fire as they ran and dived through the havoc. Reaching the middle of the road, they had nowhere to hide as a volley of shots from the rebel gunmen found their aim, and the policeman collapsed onto the ground, their smart green uniforms spattered in blood and dust. Behind them, all that was left of the burning police barracks glowed brightly in the morning dawn. The Column had done their devilish work and it was time to move on to whichever target was in the path of the fighting men.

*

Sgt. Collins was awoken by heavy thuds of footfalls coming up the barrack stairs to his sleeping quarters. "You have an urgent telephone call from Omagh," said the constable, the Sgt. could see that his ashen face was full of worry. Collins shot up quickly from his slumber and bolted down barefoot in his pyjamas to take this most urgent call. He stood quietly and listened intently to the story unfolding a few miles away in Gortin.

"Men," he said calmly, "I'm leaving you here in the barracks. The County Inspector has ordered me to take charge of a platoon of constables from Omagh, and go to Gortin Glen, the IRA is on the move in Tyrone and Derry and it looks like a major offensive, so best get your guns out and get ready to defend the barracks! I'm going upstairs to get into my uniform; I'm taking the car to Omagh to find out what is happening." Collins ran upstairs to get dressed, with his uniform on he hurried downstairs and hurried into the car.

"Driver get me to Omagh as soon as possible," he ordered, and, at that, the car was soon speeding out of the village, leaving a trail of dust behind it.

Collins arrived in time for the meeting, which was being held in the large room of the barracks. A tall, thin Army officer stood holding a wooden cane, a large map of Tyrone hung behind him on the wall.

"Good morning gentlemen," he said in a posh English public-school accent. "My name is Major General Ernest Authur Wimberley, of the 1st Battalion, South Staffordshire Regiment. I will be your commanding officer for this operation today, I won't keep you here too long, we must press on with our objective immediately." Collins sat and listened.

"Under my command will be soldiers from my own South Staffordshire regiment, and troops from the East Lancashire Regiment, men from the RIC and the Ulster Special Constabulary." He turned to his map and stretched out his arm, pointing his cane at specific parts of the map. "The 2nd Northern Division of the IRA have started this offensive, they have come down from the Sperrin Mountains at this point here, and have attacked the RIC Barracks in Gortin, killing eight policemen. Our job now is to take the fight to the enemy, and kill or capture them!" Collins raised his hand.

"Sorry sir but what is the strength of the rebel force that is on the move?" he asked.

"Thank you Sgt., that is a good question," said Wimberley. "We think the IRA have 300 or so members on the attack, and we also think they are moving on Omagh, our job will be to meet them head on, before they reach the town. Remember the tactics we need to use for the lorry convoys, it is evident to us that lorry convoys must consist of not less than six lorries, with a suitable escort to avoid all vehicles being ambushed simultaneously, these lorries must be divided into two or more groups which need to move at 300 or 400 yards apart, and part of the escort will drive between each group. If we get ambushed then the other group can stop and counterattack the ambushers." Wimberley placed the wooden cane with great care against the wall. "Right men the lecture is finished, the time for talking is over, it's now time for action and let's give these rebel scoundrels a bloody good bashing!"

The sounds of chairs scraping the stone floor echoed around the building, as the combined police and military force made their way outside to the waiting lorries at the front of the barracks. Before they embarked into the Crossley lorry, Collins had his chance to speak to the six policemen under his command, they stood to attention in front of him. "Boys, this isn't going to be pleasant, hopefully we will get through today. I think the soldiers and Special Constables will do the bulk of the fighting, so we have a good chance of making it."

Constables Finnerty from Limerick, Riordan from Kilkenny, O' Brien from Wexford, Mc Gee from Galway, along with Constables Mc Donnell and O' Connell, both from Tipperary, all climbed aboard the lorry in the warm sunshine, ready to take the fight to the rebels. Intelligence had indicated that the IRA had rested in a group of farms just outside Gortin, there was also a dugout in the same locality, but they did not know exactly where. It was, therefore arranged for the combined operation force of Military, RIC, and Ulster Special Constabulary to be dropped off from the lorries a few miles away from the enemy, so as not to disturb them, they were to march the five or so miles, and wait in position for zero hour.

A skeleton force would then drive towards the area where the IRA were waiting, then spring the trap on them. Collins and his policemen were in the last lorry on the road, he felt scared and nervous for the first time. "This is deadly work today, boys, say a prayer that we all get through it," he said, all the constables in the lorry gripped their rifles tightly in anticipation, then a huge explosion ripped through the first lorry, blasting men and body parts into the air. It turns out that the IRA had a surprise for them also. "Get to fuck out of the lorry and make for the field!" shouted a frightened Collins, as they jumped out and ran for the safety of the field.

The men huddled near their sergeant and nodded to each other in turn. "Stay low," he barked. The IRA Flying Column held a position on the high ground above the road, lead bullets rained down on the soldiers further up the lane, they fired back upward, blindly but at least still returning fire. Men on both sides collapsed and fell, covered in blood, wounded or dead, and all that was left of the first lorry burned fiercely, its acrid black smoke bellowed skywards in an angry assent. The IRA men got up from their positions and began to make their way forward towards where Collins and his men lay.

"Get up and run boys, fall back!" Collins shouted. "Fall back go, go! go! go!" He watched soldiers run past him in total disarray, and in full retreat, sprinting in fear, away from the danger, they all got through the hedges and ran for their lives, as the trench-coated enemy lobbed mills bombs at them, and continued to fire their rifles at the fleeing columns of green, black, and khaki. Guns were blasting, making muzzle bursts that punched holes in men and missed shots that lifted clumps of earth around them. The two Tipperary constables, Mc Donnell and O' Connell, fell down dead, both men shot violently in the back, the rest of the men reached the safety of a stonewall and dived over it. Suddenly the soldiers, who had made it on foot earlier, emerged from the nearby trees to counterattack the attacker's hot fiery metal. Projectiles streamed towards the IRA column, cutting men down in full flow, it was then their turn to run from the danger. The soldiers opened fire with their heavy Lewis guns, pounding the escaping attackers with a storm of bullets. As they fled back towards higher ground, the sounds of machine-gun chatter could be heard around the countryside. Collins lay and watched; he was frightened but hid his feelings from the surviving policemen under his command. A further column of Specials and soldiers moved forward on the attack; the aim was to kill or capture the IRA men, who now were scurrying in full retreat towards the safe high ground. A small group of them lay on the ground firing and providing cover for the rest of their comrades, who were now sprinting towards the cover of the trees, and the safety of the mountains. The battle was over, and Collins raised his hand, it was trembling slightly, the Tyrone countryside was a terrible landscape of death and destruction, the bodies of the dead lay on the soft green grass.

What a horrible view, he thought. War is murder, sheer bloody murder, it is well that war is so terrible – lest we should grow too fond of it. The IRA offensive had failed for different reasons, the five Northern Divisions decided to attack Northern Ireland at different times rather than attack at the same time. The 1st Northern Division of the IRA based in County Donegal was totally embroiled in a vicious internal conflict, and was so bitterly divided, it was no help to the 2nd Northern Division, which had to go it alone on the offensive. The 3rd Northern Division which covered Antrim and North Down began its failed offensive later on in the month, and by that time the 2nd Division had already collapsed. The 4th and 5th Divisions which covered Armagh, Monaghan, Cavan, and South Down, for some unexplained reason, did not go into action at all.

The May rebellion had failed, the quest for unity within the IRA had also failed and the slide to civil war in the Irish Free State was getting closer. The *new* state of Northern Ireland was saved by the infighting and division caused by the treaty, within the ranks of the IRA, and by the hard, tough men of the Ulster Special Constabulary who, by their actions, saved the Northern government and country from being an all-Ireland Republic.

CHAPTER TWENTY-FOUR

Father John Mc Chesney opened the window to see who was knocking the front door of the parochial house in such a loud and aggressive manner. Four Special Constables stood on the doorstep.

"Father Mc Chesney, get out of bed and come out here now!" they ordered.

"I'm sorry gentlemen but I have to say mass in an hour, what is the problem?" he asked.

"You can forget mass, it's all mumbo jumbo, it doesn't count for anything. The stone bridge outside the village has been damaged in a bomb attack, you and some of your Catholic residents will have to come and fix it!" they said. Father Mc Chesney got up and dressed quickly, he went outside to find a lorry waiting with shovels stacked on board, and a few of his church members sitting on back. He was bundled roughly with the rest of them, onto the vehicle, they rumbled off in the direction of the explosion.

Reaching the bridge, they were ordered off and handed the shovels.

"Get to work, we want this sorted out soon," said a Special Constable. The explosion had caused serious damage to the mouth of the devastated stone bridge. "Get to work!" another Special screamed in anger, and everyone started digging with fear, trying their best, but without any hope of filling in the yawning gap. The sound of metal on stone carried in the air and nobody said a word as they toiled in the bright sunlight. It was a waste of time doing this job as it would need a specialist gang of navvies to sort this man-made mess out. Father Mc Chesney stopped shovelling.

"Constable I must protest, but there is no way we can fix this, it's just too badly bombed," he said, the answer was immediate;

"Priest, I will be the judge of that, you and the rest of your Pope heads will keep working until we say when to stop!" Then he walked over to him and stuck his rifle barrel right into Mc Chesney's rib cage. The digging continued in a state of fear and loathing, and nobody, not even the parish priest, spoke out of turn again. When the humiliation was complete, the Special Constables took the shovels off them and put them back on the lorry.

"Sorry boys," they smirked, "we don't have any room to bring you back, you will all have to walk home." The lorry roared off, leaving Father Mc Chesney and the others stranded miles from the village. On the way back they meet Sgt. Collins alone on a bicycle patrol.

"What happened to you men?" he asked.

"We were taken from our homes and brought out here to try and mend the bridge that got blown up by the IRA," said Father Mc Chesney. Collins shook his head.

"I can't see what that was going to achieve," he said, "other than to make an example of you, but for what purpose?"

"Well, how about you tell me, Sergeant, after all, they are your men," said Father Mc Chesney angrily.

"Well I didn't tell them to behave like this. I will get back to the barracks straight away and speak to them, it is my duty to confront wrongdoing. Even if they are in uniform, my men are still subject to the law of the land!" Collins turns around and cycles with haste back to the village. "I will sort this out now!"

The men are all sat together in the main office, smoking cigarettes when Collins storms in. "What exactly is the meaning of this? Just why did you bring Father Mc Chesney and some of his flock out to fix the bomb damage today?" The men sat in pensive mood.

"Calm down, Sgt," said Hall, "they needed to be taught a lesson, you can't go around blowing things up and get away with it, and as for that black crow Mc Chesney, well the less said about him the better, we think he is a rebel supporter!"

"So you think he is a rebel supporter, my God, thinking is not a reason to harass him."

"We will do more than harass him; if we find out that it's true!" said Hall with menace.

"I just can't win with you lot, I'm going to my office, if you need me just shout," replies Collins. He walks in through the door to the safety and sanctuary of the only place left that he feels safe. On entering the room he is met by a strange sight, a huge orange arch hung over the desk and an orange flag on the wall. He turns and calls the men to the door. "What is this all about, men?" They all come over to the door and peer in to see what was happening.

"I don't know who did this, sir," said Hall, laughing, "I will remove it straight away." Collins was rattled but he didn't show it. "Somebody must be playing a joke on you, sir," said Hall. "Laird and Morton remove these items now as we certainly don't want the sergeant to be offended, it won't offend us, but I mean we all know that he is a different religion than us." The orange flag and arch were taken down with great care and placed in an old wooden box out of the view of the deeply offended Collins.

"Men carry on your duty, I want you to get out on patrol in the motor car, I'm going to walk the beat on the main street alone." And with this he walks outside to perform yet another duty in solitude. He gets just halfway down the street when a big shiny motor car pulls up and the door opens, it was Lord Copeland and his driver.

"Sgt. Collins please get in; I want you to come with me," said Copeland. Collins climbs into the car. "Now I want you to come back to my house with me as there is something we need to talk about," he said.

"Grand so," said Collins and the car speeds off towards Copeland's sprawling estate.

Copeland and Collins sit at each end of the fabulous ornate dining table in the main room of Copeland's mansion. His butler pours both men a glass of wine.

"You know why I wanted to speak to you, Sgt. Collins?"

"I have no idea Lord Copeland, please explain why, sir."

Copeland puts the glass to his lips and lightly sips the wine. "Well Sgt. you know that the 1922 constabulary of Ireland was discussed in our Northern Ireland parliament at Belfast City Hall and we agreed to disband the RIC, well tomorrow, on the 1st of June, a new police force comes into effect in the six plantation counties of Northern Ireland. It will be called the Royal Ulster Constabulary." Collins sat and listened, Copeland handed him a brown, official envelope and Collins placed it on the table next to the wine glass.

"Go on sir, have you more to say?"

"Yes," said Copeland, "I will continue, our cabinet ministers don't like the idea of too many RIC men joining the RUC as we would rather have Ulster Special Constables and officers join the new force." Collins looked puzzled.

"Why do you not want serving RIC men to join the RUC, is it because most are Catholics and from the south of Ireland just like me?" he asked.

"Well, it's one reason," he said, "but it is not the main reason."

"That's nonsense sir, I think the religion bit is exactly the reason." Copeland wasn't happy with what he said.

"I'm going to get to the point, Sgt. Collins, open the envelope now." He took a knife off the table and cut the paper open, he took out the contents and began to read the letter. A five-pound note fell onto the table, after reading he put it back next to the fiver.

"Now I want you to tell me yourself, Lord Copeland, in your own words."

"Very well, Collins, I want you to resign and leave Sixmilecross for good, I have booked you a train ticket to Belfast and also booked you a berth on the Belfast to Liverpool steamship with five pounds to start you up afresh in England."

Collins gets up from the table. "Do you honestly think that you can buy me with five pounds, five pounds!" he exclaimed. "You could put one hundred pounds or one thousand pounds on the table and you still couldn't buy me. I'm staying in Sixmilecross! A policeman is a policeman no matter what politician or government is in charge, here or indeed in any country in the world. No sir, I cannot change my principles ever! I'm well aware that every politician that has ever lived has never had any principles! Now I must quote the man that you all seem to think is related to me, Michael Collins, when he said: 'To be a politician is to say one thing and mean the other.' Now, good day to you, Lord Copeland, I will let myself out!" Collins walks towards the door of the room and hurries outside to Copeland's driver who is waiting to take him back to the village.

1ST JUNE 1922 – THE ROYAL ULSTER CONSTABULARY TAKES CONTROL.

In May the Parliament of Northern Ireland passed the 1922 Constabulary Act, the Royal Irish Constabulary was disbanded in Northern Ireland and recruitment commenced for a new police force the Royal Ulster Constabulary [RUC]. The rundown of the RIC in Ireland had commenced with immediate effect from the 27th of March and today, the 1st of June, the RUC officially came into existence with its Headquarters in Atlantic Building, Waring Street, Belfast. The green uniform, insignia and rank structure were the same to those of the RIC. The new force consisted of 3,000 men; of the 1,100 of the old RIC who were accepted 400 were Catholics, of which Sgt. Collins was one. But mostly the former members of the Ulster Special Constabulary made the transition into the RUC just as Lord Copeland had planned.

Collins stands outside the barracks, watching the workmen remove the old RIC sign from above the door and put the new sign in place. He thinks back to what he said to Lord Copeland again: "A policeman is a policeman no matter what government is in charge." One of the workmen turns to him.

"Well Sergeant how do you feel now?"

"Yesterday I was an RIC man, today I'm an RUC

man," he says. But in my heart and soul I will always be an RIC man, until the day I die, he thought to himself. He then goes inside to fill out his reports and it felt strange for him to be sending them to Belfast, rather than Dublin, but it was more proof that he now lived in a new country.

CHAPTER TWENTY-FIVE

SIXMILECROSS, NORTHERN IRELAND

TUESDAY 22ND AUGUST 1922, 10.15 P.M.

The darkness of the late August evening had arrived. Father McChesney was in the Parish House, he had just sat down when he heard a noise from outside near the front door. "Father McChesney please help me, please help." A man limped up to the door, he was in pain and discomfort as he stumbled towards the main archway. He was wearing a brown tweed jacket that was dirtied and slightly stained with blood, the man collapsed on the clean grey step. Hearing the cries for help the smartly dressed priest ran down to the hallway to give assistance, he opened the door and leaned over the prone body on the step.

"Father," said the injured man, "do you know anything about trains?" Father McChesney looked surprised.

"That is a stupid question at a time like this, are you hurt?" The man raised a Mauser pistol hidden in his coat and pointed it at the priest. McChesney had no time to react. The man's finger squeezed the trigger and hot rounds of metal slammed into the priest, creating a bloody stitchwork pattern which appeared across the black Roman Cassock he was wearing. Father McChesney tumbled backwards, he was dead before he hit the ground. His killer stood up and stared at his lifeless body.

"That is revenge for the attack on the troop train last year. You were in the group that planted the mines on the track. And Father, even though you're dead, I want you to know who I am. My name is Alexander Jackson and in the name of the Loyalist People we have got our revenge." Alexander Jackson brushed the mud and blood from his jacket and calmly walked away from the house into the dark August night.

SIXMILECROSS, NORTHERN IRELAND
TUESDAY 22ND AUGUST 1922, 11.40 P.M.

The Crossley arrived at the front of the barracks and Collins and his men pull the body of Father McChesney out from the floor of the car so they could carry him into the barracks. Standing at the door to meet them was Lord Copeland and Reverend Smythe who had just been released from the custody of the Monaghan IRA that very day. Both men looked quite happy.

"Gentlemen I heard about the shooting of Father McChesney and we just came down to see if it is true," said Copeland.

"Here is his body now," said Collins. "Do you want to come in and get a good look?"

"N, no," said Copeland, "that will not be necessary, we can view him as you bring him into the barracks." Sergeant Collins was no fan of the priest but he was slightly miffed at Copeland and Smythe coming into the village at this time of night to be nosey or, worse again, have a bit of a gloat.

Lord Copeland produced a bottle of whiskey from his coat and Smythe produced about five small thimble-sized glasses from his coat also.

"Gentlemen when you put the body inside I will invite you out for a small drink, it is a celebration." Copeland opened the bottle. "We have three things to celebrate; Reverend Smythe was released today, Father McChesney is no longer with us, and we think Michael Collins is dead but we are not sure." The men cheered.

"Michael Collins is dead; we will drink to that." The body was placed into the back room for the doctor to inspect it later when he was finished his nightly rounds. Lord Copeland, Reverend Smythe, Sergeant Collins, and the constables went back outside the barracks.

"You will excuse me if I don't join you in celebration but I could still do with a good stiff drink now so I will join you for that," said Sergeant Collins. He drank the whiskey straight down in one gulp. "Fill her up, Reverend," he said as he handed him back the glass. The glass was filled for a second time and Sergeant Collins did the same routine. "I will go back inside, men. I will see you back in the barracks whenever you are ready." Copeland and Smythe stood talking to the constables for a few more minutes but soon it was time for them to leave.

"Gentlemen I will bid you goodnight," said Copeland. His motor car and driver soon pulled up outside the barracks and both men got in. The car drove off down the main street of the village towards Lord Copeland's estate on the far side of the village. The car stopped on the darkened laneway at the edge of town. A man was standing at the side of the road. It was Alexander Jackson – he got into Lord Copeland's car and it hurried away into the night.

CHAPTER TWENTY-SIX

SIXMILECROSS, NORTHERN IRELAND

THURSDAY 28TH SEPTEMBER 1922, 10 A.M.

The morning was warm and sunny. Collins came into the public office, the night duty men were getting changed out of their uniforms and into smart suits, they also were putting on their orange sashes. Today is Ulster Day, 28th of September – the 10th anniversary of the signing of the Ulster Covenant in 1912. Lord Copeland has invited Orange lodges and marching bands from all over Tyrone and other parts of Northern Ireland to join him in celebration in his home village.

"Good morning men," he said. The men were in great spirits, they had taken turns to sleep and stay on watch. It was a quiet night for police work so they all took turns in getting a few hours' sleep to be ready for today's grand parade. Sergeant Collins walked out of the door of the Barracks and down the front steps, he turned round and saw that theBuilding was decked out in red, white, and blue bunting and each window had a Union flag and Ulster flag flying on poles from them. The main street of the village was also decked out in bunting and flags – today's parade was going to be a special event. He walked down the main street towards the railway station, trains were arriving with men and women on board, the sounds of flutes playing independently in practice filled the air. He reached the station to see the passengers get out of their carriages and walk along the platform, men in sashes and different marching band uniforms mingled along the rest of the platform and out onto the street.

Lord Copeland arrived in his car to welcome his fellow Orange brethren and Unionists to his village. He is wearing his sash, bowler hat, and smart white gloves. "I welcome you all to the village on this fine day to celebrate Ulster Day." They all assembled outside the Orange Hall across the road from the train station. The marching bands got into formation and the large orange banner depicting scenes from the Bible and Ulster history were unfurled. The lead band started playing the sash and the other marching bands began to play Derry's walls, the parade was on the move down the main street of the village with the music playing. Lambeg drummers had joined up, beating the large drums loudly. Collins walked alongside the parade on the footpath through the crowds of spectators assembled along the route. He stopped and stood in the doorway of a shop, the parade made its way along the main street and out of the village towards the field at the bottom of the road. In the field there will be a religious church service. For now Collins' job was done; he went back to the barracks for a cup of tea and a quick look over his paperwork before the parade came back to the village in a few hours. The march was peaceful and Collins laughed to himself, he was the only Catholic in town. Nobody would dare disrupt an Orange parade, all the Catholic people were gone away for the day or not coming out of their houses until it was all over.

SIXMILECROSS, NORTHERN IRELAND
28TH SEPTEMBER 1922, ULSTER DAY, 4 P.M.

Sergeant Collins sat at his desk pouring over the large amount of paperwork that had to be completed. He could hear the sound of drums and music in the distance. The Ulster Day parade was returning to the village from the bottom field. He left the work he was doing and put his tunic and belt back on, it was time to go back out on duty for the end of the parade. He walked outside into the street and walked towards the returning noise and thundering music. LoRd Copeland and Reverend Smythe led the procession, proudly both wearing their smart Orange sashes, the marchers bedecked in flags wearing other Orange symbolism and regalia. The parade led in triumph up the main street of the village. Collins stood at the middle of the street and watched the parade pass by. All the marchers were dressed smartly and were slightly boisterous but always well behaved, the event was not a temperance parade, any alcohol was limited but not banned completely. There is never any trouble at Orange parades in the countryside and the organizers, to their credit, always policed the event themselves.

1922 was becoming more peaceful as the year went on. The march finally ended up back at the village Orange Hall. Collins had walked up the street and was standing watching the marchers unwind across the road from the Orange Hall next to the train station. Lord Copeland spoke to the crowd.

"Many thanks to all my Orange and Unionist brethren for making the journey to Sixmilecross for Ulster Day. We now have a country of our own which we call Northern Ireland, we have had a wonderful and peaceful day today at our parade but remember the Devil's work is never done so we much stay vigilant for our enemies will do their best to destroy what we have achieved, so, in the words of a great British patriot Oliver Cromwell, 'Put your trust in God and keep your powder dry'." The crowd cheered and burst into song – *God Save Our Gracious King*. Lord Copeland and Rev Smythe sang along with the crowd too. Collins stood and watched the marchers unfurl the big banners which were carried on the parade. They packed everything up without any fuss and clambered back onto the waiting train. He watched the train glide from the station, chugging and hissing as it went, and he made his way back to the barracks. It was a peaceful, quiet, and thankfully uneventful day for the very few police on duty.

CHAPTER TWENTY-SEVEN

Sergeant Collins and his men were waiting to be briefed in the barracks' public office. They were told to be in full uniform and have all their full equipment on. They stood with rifles, pistols, and bandoliers, all stuffed with bullets. A big operation was underway; nobody was to be told anything until the District Inspector had arrived to brief them from Dungannon RUC Barracks. Nobody was talking, the mood was quite gloomy, nobody knew what was happening. Through the darkness they could see cars and trucks coming down the main street. "Get ready, men, this is the Inspector coming now I'd say." The cars and lorries drove up the main street and screeched to a halt outside the barracks, their doors opened and slammed shut again and men got out and came straight into the barracks.

"Good morning Sergeant, I am Inspector Campbell. There will be no pleasantries or handshakes." He took a big scroll of paper from his coat and rolled it open like a town crier about to read an important message. "I have been instructed to read out this following statement from the Government of Northern Ireland in Belfast." He looked down at the paper again. "The Civil Authorities Special Powers Act Northern Ireland 1922. This act is to enable the Government of Northern Ireland to maintain and preserve the peace of Northern Ireland. I here by decree that all Catholic men between the ages of 16 and 60 will be arrested without trial and taken to a prison to be detained until further notice. It is your job this morning starting at 5 a.m. to go to the homes of these men and arrest them. I am calling this plan Operation Roundup. Good luck, men." Sergeant Collins put his hand up.

"Sir the barracks won't hold all those people."

"Ah Sergeant I forgot to tell you, bring them to the railway station – we will then escort them by train to the Crumlin Road Jail in Belfast and there is a prison ship in Belfast lough called the Argenta and we will also intern them in Larne workhouse and Derry Gaol. Good luck, men, happy hunting." Sergeant Collins and his men climbed into the Crossleys and went in search of their quarry.

SIXMILECROSS, NORTHERN IRELAND
MONDAY 9TH OCTOBER 1922, 5 A.M.

Sergeant Collins and his men jumped out of the Crossley's. They went round the rural homes hammering and kicking on all the doors and rousing all the occupants awake in the darkness of the morning. "Everybody up out of bed now," they roared. Women still in their nightshirts screeched and screamed. The doors were kicked in and the men pulled from their beds. "Outside now, get dressed and get outside now." Sergeant Collins stood in the doorway watching the spectacle unfold. Loud shouts and screams filled the air. A military lorry pulled up outside the cottage and every man that was arrested was put in the truck and soldiers were on hand to guard them.

The same scenes were unfolding this morning at 5 a.m. all over Northern Ireland, from Belfast, Enniskillen, Omagh, and Armagh the Catholic Nationalist male population that could be a threat to the new Northern Ireland state were being rounded up and sent to jail, internment without trial under the 1922 special powers act was in full swing and underway. When Collins and his men, the soldiers, and the prisoners got back to Sixmilecross, the village was teeming with more of the same scenes. The prisoners were pulled out of the lorries and herded towards the train station. "On you get,' said a soldier, "you're going to Belfast." The prisoners were given some bread and tea and put into the carriages. There was no need to take their names, they were all known as Catholic in the region. They would be processed in Belfast when they arrived there. The sun was up, it was mid-afternoon, and the trains with internees were still passing through the village. Sergeant Collins stood on the platform watching them pass by, it was hard work but hopefully it will stop any more trouble in Northern Ireland, he thought.

CHAPTER TWENTY-EIGHT

A wet, damp winter's day. Sergeant Collins and his men arrive in the town of Strabane in another part of Tyrone, their job is to guard the border. Ireland had become two states: the Irish Free State with dominion status like Canada, and Northern Ireland which remained part of the United Kingdom and the British Empire. Collins got off the train in Strabane station. He had three other constables with him from Sixmilecross Barracks. RUC HQ in Belfast had to guard the entire length of the new border from Londonderry all the way to Newry in County Down. They had a plan to rotate police from barracks all over Northern Ireland to strong points close to the Irish Free State, it was the turn of Sixmilecross Barracks to send a sergeant and some constables to watch for any armed incursions into Northern Ireland. Sergeant Collins walked to Strabane RUC Barracks from the train station. A constable and sergeant were standing in the front door of the barracks. When they finally arrived the sergeant reached out his hand to Collins.

"Sergeant John West is my name."

"I am Sergeant Collins. We have just arrived from Sixmilecross," was his reply. "Sergeant West, what is this side of the line, or, I mean border, like?"

"It is grand, to be honest all we have to do is to guard the railway bridge from Strabane to Lifford and do a number of patrols in out motor cars on the roads around the town. It has been very quiet our side of the border since the big round up last month. Anybody that wasn't lifted in the raids are over on the Free State side of the border fighting for or against the Free State Army, they have split into two factions. You will be alright, Sergeant Collins, our only danger now is stray rounds coming our way from the other side of the border." The patrol climbed into their Crossley's and drove to the railway bridge crossing. "We don't stop any trains coming from either Lifford or Strabane, we are just on the lookout for suspicious activity. Our main worry was the Free State Army trying to cross the border, we could deal with anti-treaty forces but the Free State forces were heavily armed. However, the Civil war in the Free State has got so bad they are no threat to Northern Ireland now."

A makeshift wooden hut has been placed at the railway bridge for the police and soldiers to shelter in from the cold November weather. The men stood behind the Crossley and listened to the distant peels of gunfire and explosions in the Donegal countryside. It sounded like claps of thunder away off in the distance, are far-off booming sound echoed from that far-off area of the Free State. Sergeant Collins stood and listened to the sounds of battle. Thank God it's not here in Tyrone, I have had three years of trouble and warfare. I have just about had enough of this madness, he thought. A few hours later the Sixmilecross police contingent were back on the train to Omagh and Sergeant Collins sat quietly staring out the window at the darkness of the evening.

That is it for me now. I am 50 years of age – I am worn out and ground down with all this violence and strife, every man has a breaking point, I think I have just reached mine. I have had enough. I think it's time to retire but I will have to move to England or Scotland. I am an Irish man who is stateless – the Free State won't want me, and Northern Ireland won't want me either. It's time to retire and move away from Ireland. On the train journey from Strabane Sergeant Collins had made up his mind – it was time for a new life and a new world.

CHAPTER TWENTY-NINE

The day was bitterly cold, dry but bathed in cold sunshine. Constable Laird was standing at the desk in the public office when Sergeant Collins came in from outside. He took off his gloves and rubbed his freezing cold hands together, trying to warm them up, he walked past the medium-sized Christmas tree that was decked out in paper bows and coloured paper. It was not in the RUC regulations to have a tree in the barracks but the men had decided to show some Christmas spirit after the tough year they had put in. Collins then walked over to the fire and stood in front of it, his hands were stretched out towards the warm glow of the flames.

"There is not much heat about today, Constable Laird," said Collins.

"No sir there is no heat at all," answered Laird. "The weather forecast has predicted snow for this evening. We will have snow for Christmas for sure," he added. Collins looked over his shoulder to Constable Laird, he was the only man in the barracks he had time for.

"You are a deeply religious man, Constable Laird, I think."

"Yes sir I believe in reading the Bible and keeping true to its word," said Laird. "I will tell you something else about today, there will be a full moon tonight, it is called a frost moon or a cold moon. It is the day after the pagan event of the winter solstice, it is the brightest the moon will be this year in the sky. It might have some meaning to the pagans of old or it could be some kind of omen tonight but, if it snows, we might not get to see it."

Collins baulked. "Believing in Christ is a good thing but the belief in omens because of a full moon tonight is just a bit silly."

"I am only going with what I read about in the newspapers but if it is a clear night it will be a great sight to see in the sky later on." Collins nodded and agreed. A car screeched to a halt outside the barracks. Collins and Laird went to the window, it was a police vehicle. Two constable got out and collected a handcuffed man from the back seat, he looked sheepish as he was ushered towards the barracks. All three men came through the door.

"What have we got here, Constable?" said Laird.

"I am Constable Bingham, and this is Constable Johnstone. The prisoner is none other than Patrick Tobin, a leading Republican and one of Eamon De Valera's top men. He is wanted for murdering two Special Constables last year in Belfast. We need you to put him in a cell until he can be transported to Crumlin Road Jail in Belfast. We will put him on trial for the murders, we have no idea why he is in Northern Ireland, it must have got too hot in the Free State for him." Constable Laird went behind the desk and gathered the large jail cell keys from the locked cupboard on the wall. Laird walked the prisoner to the cell and Tobin walked in and sat down on the stone bed; Laird locked the cell door. Constable Bingham and Johnstone walked back to the front door.

"Keep the prisoner here until we get back. We will escort him on the train to Belfast, but we have other duties to attend to." Both men walked out the door, leaving Collins and Laird to guard the prisoner. Collins went back to his sergeant's office and left Laird at the public office. Laird locked the front door. If anybody wanted into the barracks, they would have to knock on the door to get in.

SIXMILECROSS, NORTHERN IRELAND
FRIDAY 22ND DECEMBER 1922, 10 A.M.

Collins sat at his desk. He was going through his paperwork but he was now worn out and run down; all he could think about was leaving his job, leaving the village and the country completely. I must go he, thought, I have to go, the time is now but how do I do it? There is a train to Belfast tonight at 11.15 p.m. Once I finish today's work then I will pack up all my things and leave. I will travel light, a case with a few items, and I will wear my best suit.

Laird knocked on the Sergeant's door. "Sergeant Collins, the prisoner is getting a bit restless, what shall I do with him?" Collins stood up.

"Get the keys, we will go in and interrogate him and find out what he is doing in Northern Ireland." Collins and Laird entered the cell. "My name is Sergeant Collins and this is Constable Laird, alright Tobin," said Collins. "I want the truth from you or else you know what will happen. Tell me why you are in Northern Ireland."

Tobin was upset. "If you must know I was trying to get to Donegal. I am a wanted man in the Free State, I killed a Free State officer in an ambush in October. The game was up for me so my only chance was to get to Donegal through Northern Ireland and catch the boat to Glasgow." Tobin got down on his knees. "Please help me, men, I can't go to Belfast they will hang me for shooting the Specials and if the Free State catch me I'll be shot in Mountjoy prison." Collins was in despair.

"Holy God is this all the Irish can do? Kill and murder each other? You can't stay in Northern Ireland, you will be hung for murder, you can't go to the Free State you will be shot for murder. My God what can you do?"

Tobin spoke again, "Sergeant Collins help me get out of this, set me free and say I escaped. Please I beg of you to help."

Constable Laird piped up, "Sergeant you should join him on the boat to Glasgow." Collins looked at Laird.

"You're mad, you think I should help this prisoner escape and catch the boat to Glasgow with him?" Tobin sat quietly, he was leaving the conversation to Laird and Collins.

"Sergeant Collins you are in a bad situation too. I am your only friend in the barracks and this village. You have a lot of enemies who most likely would want you dead too, this could be your only opportunity to get away. I will get you to tie me up and I will say we were overpowered by the prisoner and he took you as a hostage and stole the Crossley."

Collins thought deeply about his situation for a few minutes. He had had enough of policing but was this the right way to go? "This situation suits both of you," said Laird. "It is like the situation was meant to happen." Collins and Tobin agreed to the plan.

"Alright Tobin here is what we will do," said Collins, "put on the handcuffs and I will drive the Crossley. If anybody asks, you're my prisoner and I am taking you to the nearest barracks. Once we cross into the Free State I will remove the handcuffs and take off my uniform. We will drive to the boat in Donegal. Laird will be tied up and put in the cell." Collins and Tobin left the barracks and climbed into the car. They drove out of the village and along the country lanes towards the Free State and freedom for both men.

SIXMILECROSS, NORTHERN IRELAND

FRIDAY 22ND DECEMBER 1922, 2 P.M.

The Crossley made its freezing cold journey from Tyrone towards the Free State. They encountered other police vehicles along the route but were never stopped and questioned. To anyone passing it was just a police and prisoner making their way to a barracks somewhere. Collins struck up the conversation first.

"So Mr Tobin I need to ask you, did you kill the Specials in Belfast and the Free State Officer too?" Collins was slightly nervous at asking this question. Tobin looked at him and Collins looked at the road ahead.

"I will not answer that directly about those three killings but I have killed other people and to tell you the truth I have had enough of it. That is why I am trying to get the boat to Glasgow. I can't live this life anymore. I am war-weary and never want to see another fight or battle again as long as I live." Collins changed tact, he asked another question;

"Where in Donegal do we catch the boat to Scotland?" asked Collins.

"From Moville and it is a way up in Northern Donegal so it will be a long enough drive to get there too," replied Tobin. As the car turned around the next corner an RUC roadblock was in place. Collins looked a bit startled, but he composed himself and spoke to Tobin.

"Let me do the talking." The Crossley stopped dead at the road block. "Hello men how are things today?"

"We are grand," answered a constable. "And who is your prisoner?" Collins stayed calm.

"This is Johnny Quinn. He was caught making poteen this morning, I am bringing him to Strabane Barracks. He is for court in the morning for making the stuff." Another constable at the roadblock spoke up.

"It's a pity you have no poteen with you now, we could all do with a drop to warm us up." Collins and Tobin laughed.

"Ah now lads if I'd have known you were out on the road this freezing cold day I would have kept some spare in my coat." All the men laughed.

"You can go on your way, Sergeant, the sooner we are all off this road and your prisoner is in jail the better." The Crossley sped off along the road. Donegal and the Free State was getting closer and closer. Around the next bend and both men were in Donegal.

"Yes, we have made it, Collins." Tobin banged his seat with delight. "We are free, FREE!" They drove on for another mile and stopped by the side of the road. "Are you forgetting something, Sergeant? Can you take my handcuffs off?" Collins took out his keys and removed the cuffs. Collins smiled.

"How far is the boat at Moville from here, Tobin?" Tobin put his arm on Collins' shoulder.

"It is about a seven hours' drive from here, we will need to ditch the Crossley at the nearest town and hide somewhere until then." Tobin reached around Collins and grabbed his revolver from his open-topped holster. "HANDS UP COLLINS!" he shouted. Collins was livid.

"You double-crossing bastard! What is the meaning of this?" Tobin was in control of the situation now.

"Don't worry I am not going to kill you; you have helped me well. I need to get back to my men in the Republican forces and take the fight to the Free State. They are hiding in the Donegal mountains. Once I find them I will set you free. We will get you to Moville too for the boat to Glasgow." Collins was fuming, he was made a total fool of by this gangster and now he is his prisoner. Tobin pointed the revolver at Sergeant Collins. "Get in the car and drive." Tobin got in the car beside Collins and pointed the gun into his stomach. "No funny stuff, Collins, or the gun goes off." They drove off again in search of Tobin's anti-treaty Republican forces.

COUNTY DONEGAL, IRISH FREE STATE

22ND DECEMBER 1922, 3 P.M.

A cold sun shone down on icy Donegal. Sergeant Collins was now the prisoner of Patrick Tobin, his own Webley revolver was wedged into his stomach, one false move and he would be shot dead. Tobin had form for being a killer and would not hesitate to pull the trigger and blow him away. Collins drove the car towards the Donegal mountains, he never spoke, he was in deep shock at how things had turned against him. He should never have went along with this plan, it was shear madness from the start, he thought, but he was desperate to get away from everything and start a new life.

"You saved me from the hangman in Northern Ireland, Collins, so I owe you that. Once I meet up with my men you will be given money and taken to Moville, that is a promise," said Tobin. Collins was scared, he did not believe him.

You fucking lied to me the first time, he thought, he could be lying now. Collins was now resigned to his fate when they meet up with the Republican forces. *I will be shot dead,* said Collins to himself. On the next bend the Crossley had to slow almost to a stop. A cart was crashed on the road and broken porter bottles were scattered all beside it. Tobin looked scared.

"Reverse the car, quick," he said, "we will go another way. GO, GO, GO!" Before he could reverse the car was surrounded by soldiers in uniform – Free State Soldiers.

"Get your fucking hands up," they shouted, and they pointed their rifles at Collins and Tobin.

"Oh, shite I am caught." A soldier pointed his rifle straight at Tobin. He could see that he was pointing a revolver sat Collins. "Drop your weapon now," he ordered. Tobin threw the gun out onto the road.

Collins spoke, "This man Patrick Tobin was being escorted to Crumlin Road Jail by the RUC when he overpowered me and took me prisoner from across the border in Tyrone." The Free State Soldiers were soon joined by their officer, he had heard everything Collins said.

"RUC man, what is your name?"

"Sergeant Collins," was the reply. The officer walked up to Tobin.

"We know who this is, boys, OC Patrick Tobin of anti-treaty forces number four brigade from Stranorlar, Donegal. He killed a Free State officer in October when he escaped from Dundalk Barracks." Tobin stood quiet. The officer spoke again. "Alright Tobin we will give you a chance, start running."

"What?" said Tobin.

"You heard me; we will give you a chance. Start running, now." Tobin bolted for the field, he sprinted as fast as he could away from the soldiers, he was running and running and was getting tired, but he pushed on. The officer pointed at his men.

"He is escaping, boys, open fire." The soldiers fired at their moving target and he fell down dead, face down in the mud. "He did not get far," said one of the soldiers. Collins did not care, he was bluffed by him and had no sympathy for him.

"Right, Sergeant, let's get you back to Tyrone. I am sure the RUC will be looking for you by now." The soldiers retrieved the dead body of Tobin and put him in their Free State Crossley and they escorted Collins in his car back to the border and County Tyrone. Collins made his way to Sixmilecross, it was getting dark and it was also starting to snow. He had some explaining to do but he would pack his suitcase and catch the 11.15 p.m. train to Belfast before his luck would run out.

SIXMILECROSS, NORTHERN IRELAND
FRIDAY 22ND DECEMBER 1922, 6 P.M.

When Sergeant Collins arrived back in Sixmilecross it was dark and snowing hard, the brightly glowing Christmas candles were shining from every window in the village, including the barracks. He pulled up outside and walked up the steps to the front door. When he walked into the public office he was met by the County Inspector and the District Inspector.

"What Happened to you?" they asked.

"I was taken prisoner and Constable Laird was tied up here and put in the cell."

"What happened to the prisoner, did he get away?" asked the County Inspector.

"We made it into Donegal and we got stopped by Free State troops. Tobin was shot dead as he tried to escape."

"I want a full report on my desk tomorrow afternoon, in Omagh, Sergeant, and if that means you need to come up to Omagh with the report then so be it," said the District Inspector. "We are both late and have a train to catch. We will see you in the morning." They both went out the door and walked down the street to catch the train at the station.

SIXMILECROSS, NORTHERN IRELAND
FRIDAY 22ND DECEMBER 1922, 7 P.M.

Fluffy flakes of snow fell from the dark sky, continuous and billowing in majestic swirls around the village and countryside. The street was empty, it had seemed that everyone in the village had decided not to brave the cold, snow-covered night but to stay at home until the heavy flakes had stopped. Sergeant Collins stared out of the second-floor window of the barracks, mesmerized by the sight of the white cottony spectacle falling outside. He had gone up to the sleeping quarters to pack his suitcase – he was leaving on the 11.15 p.m. train to Belfast for sure; he would not change his mind, he was leaving the police, the village, and Ireland – both Free state and

Northern Ireland – forever. He was not going to tell anybody, he would just leave his letter of resignation to be found at the front desk in the public office. He filled the suitcase with the clothing he needed, he shut it closed and placed it in the corner beside the bed. Sergeant Collins lay down on his barracks bed for the last time and straight away he fell off to sleep. It had been another day of misery and he was shattered with today's troubled experience.

The clock in the hall began to chime, Ding Bong Bong! 10.45 p.m. was the time. Sergeant Collins was woken by the chimes. He got quickly up from the bed and went to the window, it had stopped snowing, everywhere was covered in untouched pristine whiteness. The large frost moon was in the sky at its brightest, bathing magnificent silvery light all over the village. Sergeant Collins went down to his office, he placed the letter of resignation on his own desk and hung up his uniform on a coat stand in the corner of the room. He placed his great coat over the tunic and placed his cap on the top of the stand. He was now ready to leave Ireland for his new life.

The barracks was quiet; nobody was needed on the front desk. In the public office the three constables on duty were in the back room typing up their individual cases of paperwork, they never noticed him going about his plan for leaving tonight. He then put his revolver into the firearms room and locked the door. The time to leave was getting closer, the train would soon be at the station. He went back up the stairs to collect his case. He would walk down to the station and wait for the train in the warm, inviting waiting room. He had one more look around the upstairs, it was time to go, but suddenly, from the corner of his eye, something caught his attention outside on the snow-covered street. A man was walking alone, nobody else was about, that was strange. He stared down at the man.

"It's Alexander Jackson, fuck me," exclaimed Collins. "He is always up to no good, he must be fresh out of Crumlin Road Jail in Belfast today." Jackson took something from his coat – it was a hammer – he went up to the front door of one of the shops and wedged the door open. His police instinct took over and Collins ran downstairs, he grabbed a police coat and cap lying in the corner of the office which belonged to another policeman and ran to the front door. He lifted a heavy brown wooden truncheon and ran to arrest Jackson. Sergeant Collins was met with the bitter cold on the barrack steps. He then followed Jackson's snow tracks to the shop that Jackson was going to rob. As Sergeant Collins came through the door he watched as Jackson broke open the till and was stuffing bank notes into his coat pocket.

"Put the money down," Collins shouted, "the game is up." Jackson spun around and fired his revolver at Collins. It caught him in the shoulder and spun him sideways, blood poured from his wound. Collins dropped the truncheon on the shop floor, it was no use anyway in a shootout. Jackson fired three more shots, hitting Collins in the side and the back, he turned and tried to run from the shop. Collins scattered the powdered snow under foot as he moved, he was covered in blood. Sergeant Collins made it halfway up the steps of the barracks, but he collapsed down and just lay bleeding in the snow. The three constables had heard the commotion and ran out. They cradled Collins as he lay dying on the street. Lights were coming on in the village, the people had heard the shooting.

It was a cold snowy moonlit December night, two days before Christmas, but Sergeant Collins had died. In his own words; "we are just shadows passing time, life is not fair and that is that."

EPILOGUE

With the murder of Sergeant Patrick Joseph Collins of the Royal Irish Constabulary, the perpetrators prospered. Constable Hall was promoted to Sergeant in the RUC, taking up the old post that belonged to Sergeant Collins. Alexander Jackson became Lord Basil Copeland's personal bodyguard, living to a ripe old age. Reverend Samuel Smythe became the local member of parliament and the grand master of the Orange Lodge for Ireland whilst Lord Basil Copeland became the longest serving Prime Minister of Northern Ireland. Politics always wins over principles.

Sergeant Patrick Joseph Collins SGT 60722 Royal Irish Constabulary, born 17th August 1872, died 22nd of December 1922, was buried quietly and in secret in Ballinhassig Catholic church on Goggins Hill, County Cork, near to the old barracks where he was to work in, when he got his promotion as head Constable in 1922, a post that was never to be filled by him or anybody else as the RIC was disbanded and a new force of the Irish free state called the Civic guard took charge of the barracks and Policing for that part of

Ireland. It was the price he had to pay for being an Irishman in the King's uniform. His earthly remains lie in an unmarked grave, unknown, forgotten, and airbrushed from history, just like the police force he proudly served in.

THE END

GOODBYE RIC

We're going away now, we're fading fast.

The splendid heroes of the past.

Some lie in graves from Leir to Loos,

brought out there by an English rose.

Some of us fell in England's cause,

in Erin's Isle maintaining laws.

Some lie in graves from Foyle to Lee,

fell fighting in the RIC.

ABOUT THE AUTHOR

David McCann from Enniskillen, Co. Fermanagh. I have an interest in Irish History and write fictional stories. I have an interest in Irish History, particularly the period from 1919-1923, from the War of Independence to the Irish Civil War. I currently have two books available on Amazon Kindle, 'The Green Fella' and 'A Boy Called Yank'.

www.ingramcontent.com/pod-product-compliance
Lightning Source LLC
Chambersburg PA
CBHW061503050726
47593CB00002B/419